First published in Great Britain in 2

Publishing

Copyright © P T Saunders 2020

Left Behind

Alex is Back

CHAPTER 1

Police Psychologist Marian Monk's office

Ted Baxter sat silently, patiently waiting, whilst the force psych quack, or Moody Monk as she was known

at the yard, flipped through his case file. She had the reputation of being a right anal bitch, who rarely passed people fit and would more commonly recommend discharge. Monk studied Ted's case file. He was waiting, no, hoping that she would give him the all clear to go back to work.

Following his suicide attempt, after seeing his ex-partner Annie Harris so brutally murdered, the Chief Super and the Commissioner had insisted that Ted attend therapy, telling him that he would remain on sick leave until the quack gave him the all clear to return to normal duties.

It was now five weeks since Annie's murder, and Ted was going out of his mind with boredom. He also needed to get that bastard Mike, or rather Alex Langdon, for killing his friend and partner, Annie.

Eventually, the middle-aged frump looked over the top of her bi-focal glasses. 'Chief Inspector Baxter,

when was the last time you took a drink?'

'A month ago, just before I started to attend the AA,' Ted lied. He'd only been to one session for about ten minutes. Ted didn't do group therapy. He'd managed to convince the group leader that it would be in his own interest to keep shtum and just mark him as present each week. That's if he wanted to be able to park anywhere in the city of London without getting a

ticket.

'Have you had any recent thoughts of suicide?' the Doctor. probed further, whilst wearing her practiced and false, sympathetic and caring smile.

'No not at all,' said Ted, sporting his own "My world's just great" smile.

In reality, Ted was still downing a few cans of Stella and a half-bottle of vodka most nights. He also thought about ending his life on an almost daily basis. The only thing stopping him from topping himself was

his need to catch and punish Annie's killer.

The quack looked down at her notes for what seemed an age to Ted. Then, she suddenly picked up one of two stamps she had sitting on an ink block in front of her and stamped a piece of paper.

'I'm declaring you fit for light duties for the next two weeks, and provided you keep off the booze and don't have any more suicidal episodes. In the meantime, I'll look at putting you on full duties at the end of those two weeks,' she said, as she handed Ted

the Fit to Work certificate.

Ted didn't hang around; he was out of her office as fast as a rat up a drainpipe. Deciding that there was no time like the present, he made his way straight to Scotland Yard, via the Old Bull public house, where he dropped in for a quick dose of Dutch Courage, which took the form of a double vodka.

Ten minutes later, Ted approached the front entrance of Scotland Yard. He hesitated for a few moments, staring up at the famous rotating Scotland Yard sign, as he thought about the last time he was inside the building. It was the morning after the night he had saved Ben Hickson – the very same night that his beautiful partner Annie Harris was horribly

slaughtered.

Ted pulled himself together and went straight to his office. Once there, he sat behind his desk and stared at the empty desk opposite him – Annie's desk. He closed his eyes and thought about the banter they'd shared, and how she was probably the only person in the Force who could get away with chastising him. 'Don't you worry Annie; I'll get the bastard who killed you. If it's the last thing I do,' he promised Annie's desk.

Ted then looked through his case files piled on his desk, then searched his filing cabinet. He was looking for the Ben Hickson files, but they weren't there. He hesitated for a few seconds, before plucking up the courage to search through Annie's desk. While he was doing that, he called Detective Jake Cummings

in the incident room.

'Incident room, Detective Cummings.'

'Jake, it's me, Ted. I'm looking for the Ben Hickson files. Any idea where they are?'

'Probably with Tingy. He took over the case when you went on sick leave. He's taken us all off the case, and has got his own team from another division working on it,' replied the detective.

'Like hell he is'. Ted shouted, slamming down the phone and storming straight to the Chief Super's office.

He burst into Max Tingy's office like a bull in a china shop.

'Ah! Ted, come in, why don't you? Don't bother knocking,' said Tingy sarcastically, clearly annoyed by Ted's interruption.

'Don't 'Ted' me. I want the Alex Langdon file, and I want my team back on the case,' Ted yelled. 'Now, now, Ted. You really do need to calm it down a little. You also need to remember who you're talking to,' replied Chief Tingy, before turning to his female guest and apologising for the interruption.

'I know who I'm speaking to, and there is no way on this earth that I'm off this case,' insisted Ted. 'Annie was my partner, and I will catch the bastard that killed her. And that, Sir, is final!'

'Calm down Ted. I have every intention of handing the Langdon case back to you. And talking of partners, meet your new partner, Detective Sergeant Carol Speakman,' said Tingy, waving his hand in the direction of the seated female detective.

'No, no way! I don't need another partner. From now on I fly solo. no offence,' Ted glanced

apologetically at Carol, who smiled and waved
away

his harsh words with a nervous smile.

'You don't have a choice. You either work with a

partner or you don't work at all,' said Tingy. The

Commissioner wants someone to keep an eye on
you after what happened, or should I say, nearly
happened

in your office a few weeks ago.'

Ted thought for a moment or two, then

reluctantly agreed to have Carole partner him.

'Good, that's sorted. I'll let you bring Detective Sgt.

Speakman up to date on the case,' said the chief,

handing the Langdon files to Ted.

Ted and Carol left the chief's office together and

headed to Ted's.

Detective Sgt. Speakman was a tall and voluptuous

Irish redhead, who looked more like a centrefold

than a detective. However, during her five years of

police service so far, Ted knew she'd been involved

in the capture of several high-ranking drug dealers,

as well as a couple of sex trafficking gangs. She was tough and up for anything, and was also the only female to ever achieve her third dad in karate.

CHAPTER 2

Waterloo Station London

After a long drive and a cross-channel train journey, Alex finally arrived at Waterloo station, having breezed through an almost non-existent border security check. Now very tired and in need of a good meal, a shower and some sleep, Alex took a taxi to the London Hilton in Park Lane.

On inspection of John-Michael's passport, the clerk on the hotel reception gave Alex a confirmatory glace and started to speak to Alex in French. Not understanding a word, Alex was forced to think on his feet. 'Can you speak in English please? After all, we are in England,' said Alex, with a smirk upon his face that told the clerk that he was in no mood to make friends or get into small talk.

The clerk took the hint and, looking rather sheepish handed Alex the key to his room 'Room 141, Sir. The second floor, on the left.'

Once in his room, Alex ordered from room service, a breakfast of eggs benedict, coffee and some tangerines. He then took a quick shower, whilst he waited for his food to arrive.

Once showered, Alex flicked through the various news channels… The woods near the villa in the south of France were still burning, and the emergency services had found a body in the burnt-out villa. The body was believed to be the body of a man wanted by both the British and Italian police, who happened to be wanted for multiple homicides in both countries. Apparently, a car that the killer had hired had been found abandoned in a multi-storey car park

in Dijon. Apparently, it had a tracker attached to it. The reporter explained that local police had carried out a number of enquiries and had learned that just over an hour or so after the car had entered the car park, an Englishman had purchased a Renault Cleo for

cash.

It was that same Renault Cleo that had been found in the garage of the burnt-out villa.

Furthermore, it was believed that the wanted man had perished in his car. The body was so badly burned, though, that it was impossible to confirm it. 'According to the local police, the man probably perished as he tried to escape the fire,' said the news anchor-man.

Alex smiled to himself. He couldn't have wished for a better outcome. Once again, Alex Landon, aka Ethan Clarke, was officially deceased, which suited him fine.

After eating his breakfast, Alex carried out a few internet searches and made a few telephone calls, before retiring to his bed. He had nothing more to do until the later evening.

Later that evening, after yet another disturbed sleep, Alex took a train to Luton. Once there he made his way to the Prince Albert public-house. It was located just outside of Luton centre and was well known as black and Asian drug dealer's paradise. The Prince

Albert was the sort of place that only the drug lords, their bitches and the desperate Wanna-be drug pushers got their supplies. It was also a no-go area for the local police, a place that, with the right contacts

and money, you could purchase anything from a 9mm

pistol to a surface-to-air missile. It was the criminal underworld equivalent of Walmart. Alex had shopped there on many occasions since his release from Afghan. In fact, it was there that Alex had purchased the explosive collar that he'd used to kill Annie XX with.

His contact, a young, black, skinny idiot and petty thief, who went by the name of Justin Justout, on account of his being either just in or just out of prison,

was already there, sitting waiting for Alex at the bar. As Alex approached, Justin jumped to his feet. 'What's happening, brother?' he said, attempting a high five with a stupid smile on his face.

Alex ignored him and ordered a Guinness from the barman. Justin looked a little confused and fell silent, waiting for Alex to respond. Once Alex got his beer, he took a seat at a table in the corner of the bar. Justin followed close behind.

'What's up with you, bro'?' Justin asked, taking the opposite seat at the table.

'Firstly, dipshit, I am not your brother. Secondly, I don't appreciate people drawing attention to the fact that I have just entered the room. The only reason you are still breathing right now is because I have a use for you. Do I make myself clear?' Alex said quietly, glaring at the young, black kid.

Justin's face suddenly lost its smile, which was replaced with a look of fear. 'All right, man. Chill,' said

Justin, visibly trying to regain a little self-respect. Alex handed him his shopping list and an envelope containing a £1000 in cash. "That's what I want, and I need it by the end of play tomorrow, let's say 6 pm. Call me when you have the items and we'll arrange a meet." Alex handed the kid his mobile number. "And one other thing, don't even think of ripping me off, or I'll hunt you down and make you wish you were dead. Alex warned, as Justin went to leave.

Alex waited for a few moments before leaving the pub himself and making his way to Oxford street.

CHAPTER 3

An underground Car Park in Victoria

Alex sat in his rented Ford Mondeo in a dimly-lit underground car park. Apart from the odd car coming and going, the place was relatively quiet. Alex knew it was never really a busy car park, as it's operator LCP had set the parking charges far too high for the locals,

relying solely on ignorant tourists for its income.

He was somewhat angered that he had been

there for almost three-quarters of an hour, waiting for that fucked-up little shit Justin. Alex could feel his adrenalin levels rising and bubbling up like poison in a witch's cauldron. His body started to shake more violently with every passing minute. Justin was supposed to have been here forty minutes ago. Where the fuck is, he? Alex detested lateness. It was unprofessional, rude and, in his experience, could lead to people getting hurt, or even dying.

He recalled a time when he and his team had been in Iraq tracking and destroying mobile scud units. They had taken out one particular rocket unit, after which they made their way to an agreed extraction point. They were on foot and being closely pursued by a unit of well-pissed-off Iraqi troops. The team arrived three minutes ahead of the designated rendezvous time. The Iraqis were about ten minutes behind, so there should have been enough time to board and be out of there before the Iraqis could get within small arms range.

But the chopper was a no-show, and they soon found themselves surrounded by about twenty-or-so Iraqi troops. The four men ended up having to fight their way out of there, losing one of the team in the process. *Fucking RAF,* Alex thought, just as he noticed Justin's Ford Ka coming down the ramp. *About fucking time, you fucking shit,* Alex muttered to himself. *And what the fuck is that you're driving?* He watched in disbelief, as the garish yellow, green and black Ford Ka drew nearer. *Talk about not drawing attention to*

yourself, Alex thought, flashing his headlights twice. As Alex stepped from his car and approached Justin's dump of a car, the kid nervously opened the boot of his Car. Laid out inside was an M16 assault rifle, a 9mm Browning with a silencer, three boxes of ammo, half-dozen detonators, some rope and a kilo of plastic explosive. Alex picked up the 9mm and began to inspect it. He removed the empty magazine. 'Rounds,' he said, holding out his hand. Justin hesitated for a few seconds; it wasn't usual protocol to load the weapon in the presence of the dealer.

However, this guy was a serious piece of work, and Justin knew it was probably not a good idea to get on the wrong side of him. He cautiously opened one of the boxes of ammo, extracted three rounds and handed them over to Alex. Justin hadn't noticed that, whilst he was getting the ammo, Alex had attached the silencer to the 9mm, then loaded the ammo into the magazine. He reached into his jacket breast pocket and pulled out a stuffed envelope, which he threw into the

Ka's boot.

'Count it,' ordered Alex, pointing to the envelope.

'It's okay, man, I trust you,' said Justin.

'Count it,' repeated Alex, with authority.

Justin did as he was told. While he counted, he failed to notice Alex cocking the 9mm and pointing the barrel at him

'It's all there,' said Justin, looked up from the

envelope of money to see Alex aiming the gun at him. Justin raised his arms in a gesture of surrender. 'Hey, bro! What are you doing? Oh, shit man, please don't do this to me, I got you what you wanted, and I can get you more anytime you like. Please don't kill me,' he begged, now a quivering wreck of a black

punk.

'Relax, I'm not going to kill you.' Said Alex, lowering the gun. 'Just transfer the stuff to my car,' he ordered, opening the boot of the Mondeo. Justin did as he was told.

'Now, just to be on the safe side, I want you to get into the boot of your car, and I need you to promise not to make a sound for at least ten minutes. Do you think you can do that, Justin?' asked Alex with a cheesy Cheshire Cat smile on his face, as he waved the 9mm toward the boot of Justin's car.

'Yes, I can do that man,' replied Justin, still shitting himself with fear, as he crammed himself into the Ka's small boot.

Once Justin was in the boot, Alex shot him twice in the head.

Sucker, he thought to himself, as he closed the boot on the now well and truly silenced Justin.

CHAPTER 4

Inspector Allocco's Office

Chief Inspector Allocco sat at his desk savouring his espresso and reviewing some case files, while Dino lounged at the desk opposite, when the phone rang. Slightly annoyed at the disturbance, Allocco answered.

'Chief Inspector Allocco...'

'Antonio, it is Marco.'

'Bon giorno, Marco.'

'I thought that I would update you on our friend Alex Langdon.'

'Hold on Marco, I'll put you on load speaker..., okay, continue,'

'Well, we have just been informed that your fugitive Alex Langdon was probably caught up in a forest fire just outside of Freijus. Apparently, he was burned to death in a car that we believe he purchased from a dealership in Dejon. It looks like your hunt for

your killer is over.'

'Has he been formally identified?' Allocco

asked.

'That, I'm afraid, is almost impossible to do with any sort of accuracy. However, it is the car your man purchased, and some documents found in the boot of the car had the names of both Ethan Clarke and Mike Travis'.

'Okay, thank you for letting me know. Please keep me informed of any further developments' said Allocco, putting the phone down.

Dino looked on in silence, as Allocco looked through the file, he had compiled on Alex Langdon.

'I guess that's case closed for us on this one,

Sir?' Dino offered.

Allocco didn't reply, but continued to read through the file, rubbing his chin from time to time.

'Sergeant, if you believe that, you are more stupid than I have given you credit for. Do you really think that someone as professional as Langdon, would actually be dumb enough to get caught out by a forest fire?'

Dino looked at his boss with a confused expression on his face, then shrugged his shoulders. 'Mark my words, Sergeant, our man is not dead, and he will kill again. The only questions are when and where. Let's hope he doesn't come back to Italy.' the chief said, as he threw Alex's file into his in tray.

CHAPTER5

Poland Street, London

Alex checked his watch as he noticed a figure heading toward the rear entrance of the Oxford Street branch of Marks and Spencer's. Eleven forty-five: obviously the changeover time for the security staff, he noted. The man entering the building was none other than David Kean, the big mouthed ex-tenant that had led the

police to Ben Hickson.

Alex knew from Kean's former tenancy agreement that he worked as a night watchman at the prestigious store.

Although that had been a while ago, and his target tonight was not that significant in the scheme of things, Kean had made Alex look a fool. To Alex that was never excusable. *Time for you pay for opening your big mouth,* Alex thought to himself, taking up his position at the back door with his trusty dagger in

hand.

He didn't have to wait long before the now off duty security guard opened the door. As it swung open, Alex leapt forward and thrust the dagger straight into the throat of the guard, dragging him back into the building before cupping his victims' mouth and nose until he was dead.

Alex could have taken Kean out at the entrance to the building, but that would have been too easy. Plus, Alex wanted to play with him a little first. Once he had stashed the body of the security guard under the stairwell, Alex made his way up the metal staircase and headed for the store's security and CCTV room. Reaching the door, he peered through the narrow glass panel. David Kean was sitting at his desk playing around with what looked to be a portable DVD player.

You perverted fucker, Alex thought to himself, as the night watchman undid his trousers once the blue movie started. Alex waited until the guard was pumping his penis frantically and about to climax, before bursting into the room and coshing Kean with his 9mm pistol. Kean went out like a light.

Even though Kean was a slim man, with as much meat on him as a butcher's pencil, Alex nevertheless struggled to drag him up the nest flight of stairs leading to the roof top.

Once there, he made a noose in the piece of rope that he had found attached to the window cleaning platform and placed it around Kean's neck. Then, he shuffled the limp body to the edge of the roof top. He paused to remove Kean's trousers and underwear, made a few cosmetic changes, and then pushed the

now-dead man over the edge of the roof.

Having sorted out his former tenant to his satisfaction, Alex exited through the building's back door and made his way back to his hotel. Once in his room, he ordered a club sandwich, a bottle of merlot and some tangerines from the room service menu, before taking a shower and brushing the metallic taste of killing from his mouth.

After eating his sandwich, Alex turned on his laptop and tuned into the French national news channel France 24. He didn't have to wait long before news of his killing of the annoying bitch Rachel came on. Apparently, the whole of the country was outraged that someone could commit such a heinous crime. Alex smiled. *Always good to be so effective as a killer.'* he thought to himself, closing the laptop and retiring to

bed.

Following another disturbing night's sleep, Alex turned on the TV and tuned into the BBC news channel. Poor David Kean's body had been discovered. It was the top news item.

'Breaking news,' said the news reporter, 'is that the body of a man in his mid-to-late forties was discovered hanging from the roof of the Marks and Spencer's building in Oxford Street today. Police say that, as a result of the man's injuries, they are treating his death as suspicious. The identity of the man is at this point unknown; however, it is believed that the store's night watchman who was on duty last night

has been reported missing.'

I can't believe they haven't found the other security guard; they must be blind, Alex thought, turning off the TV.

CHAPTER 6

Alex's room and the Hilton

Back at Scotland Yard, Ted sat at his desk, busily re-acquainting himself with the with the

Langdon file. His phone rang.

'Inspector Baxter.'

'Ted? It's Jake. You need to come up to the incident room asap. Our man's back and he wants us to know it.'

'I'll be right there,' said Ted, replacing the receiver and grabbing his jacket. He looked over at Carol, who sat looking at him like a little puppy waiting for permission to join its master.

'You'd better come, too' he told the red-headed detective sergeant.

'Right behind you, boss,' she replied, eagerly leaping out of her chair.

'Don't call me boss, the name is Ted.' Ted said,

as he held the door open for his new partner.

Once in the incident room and following Ted's introduction of his new partner, Jake brought him and Carol up to date on the new case that was unfolding.

'A man was found hanging from the roof of the Marks and Spencer's store in Oxford Street at seven this morning. A couple of cops from the City of London police attended the scene and found this attached to the roof's railings, 'said Jake, handing Ted
a note.

Ted read the note.

'Hi Ted, have you missed me. Guess who's next? See you soon. Alex,' it said.

'Ted, the guy found hanging from the building was one David Kean, the ex-tenant of Alex Langdon, the one who led us to the whereabouts of Ben Hickson.'

'I know who he is Jake. How could I forget?'

Ted said, studying the note.

Jake then took some photos from and envelope and warned the female detective, 'You may want to turn away,', as laid them on the table to reveal the shocking images.

Alex had given Kean a Columbian neck-tie, and had also castrated him and stuffed his testicles and penis into his mouth. Carol retched at the sight of the victim, but managed to keep it in. 'Welcome to homicide,' said Ted, as he handed the photos to his partner. 'Pin them up.'

'There's more. Ted. The locals found another security guard who'd been stabbed in the throat and is close to death. He's now under armed guard at the Royal Free. It's touch and go as to whether he'll make it. I've sent a couple of our guys over there to see if we

can get a description of his assailant.'

'Good work, Jake. I think we'd better let our friend Ben Hickson know that his old pal Alex is back. Get him to a safe house asap, and let me know when he's secure. Keep the details of where you put him between the three of us for now.'

'What about you, Ted? Sounds as if he's looking to take care of you too.' Jake said.

'Don't worry about me, just get to Ben, and be quick about it,' replied Ted.

'Wilko,' Jake said, exiting the room.

'Sergeant, call down to the SISI's office and get hold of Danny. Tell him to meet me in my office asap. And get me a coffee on your way back. Black no sugar.' ordered Ted, leaving the ops room.

Back in his office, Ted was joined by Danny, Carol and Bob Griffiths, the press liaison rep.

Once Ted had brought them all up to date, he told Bob to release the details of the second security guard, hoping to draw Langdon out; if he thought the guard might be able to identify him, Langdon might

attempt to shut him up permanently.

Ted ordered Danny and his team to gather and scrutinise all available CCTV from Oxford Street and Portland Road. In addition, he requested that Danny fit tracker devices to all the team's personal phones and cars, and get extra batteries for the team's mobile

phones. He wasn't about to let another partner down.

'What about me?' Carol asked, cautiously.

'I need you to liaise with Jake. And once he's got Ben settled, you and Jake can take it turns to babysit him. Twelve hours on and twelve off. I'm off to Marks and Sparks. Keep me informed.' Ted said, as he went in search of his friend and driver Sergeant Pete Machin.

CHAPTER 7

The Safe House, No. 12 Beverley Gardens

Jake, Ben and a couple of armed plain-clothed TSG guys, arrived at the safe house. It was a traditional four-bed semi with an integral garage, which was fitted with an electric up-and over-door. The house was located in the Golder's Green area of London. It had been used as a safe house on a few occasions in recent years. To date, it had provided a highly successful means for protecting witnesses.

Several external CCTV cameras covered a 360-degree radius of the house. There were also alarm mats scattered around the garden and on the front and back door steps.

'This is the best place for you right now. It's like Fort Knox,' Jake reassured Ben, as they made themselves comfortable in the sparsely furnished lounge.

'You don't know Alex Langdon like I do. Nowhere is impenetrable to him. He's a professional psychopath,' said Ben, pouring himself a whisky to calm his nerves.

Jake briefed the TSG guys on the password for entry, 'Name that bird,' to which the visitor should reply cuckoo, cuckoo. He instructed them on a change-over every eight hours, stressing that Alex Langdon was an extremely capable individual, who wouldn't think twice about killing them. 'Keep your wits about you at all times.' He told the team, before sending Ted a text: 'Cuckoo in the nest and all is well,' it said. He then sent Carol a text containing a shopping list. The only supplies they'd found in the kitchen were a couple of tea bags, some coffee stained sugar and two half-bottles of brown and red sauce.

An hour or so later, Jake spotted Carol's car turning onto the driveway. She was loaded down with several carrier bags of shopping. *At last, my stomach thinks my throat has been cut,* he thought to himself, as he rushed to open the door for her.

'I hope you've got some decent grub. I'm bloody starving,' he said, relieving her of a couple of the loaded carrier bags.

'What happened to using the password?' Carol asked, watching Jake dash into the kitchen whilst rummaging through the shopping, like a child with its

presents on Christmas morning.

'I could see it was you on the CCTV monitor,' replied Jake, still busy rummaging through the provisions she'd bought.

'There should be enough to last a few days or

so,' she said, as she followed Jake into the kitchen.

'You look more like a hungry puppy than a detective,' she quipped Carol, wrestling some of the bags of shopping from Jake.

'So, what's for dinner then?' Jake wanted to know, as he delved into a bag of crisps.

'Whatever you want to cook yourself,' replied

Carol, stealing some of Jake's crisps before she left.

Jake watched on the CCTV monitor as Carol got into her car and drove off.

A few seconds later, Ben walked into the room.

'So, what's for dinner then Sgt?'

'Whatever you want to cook yourself,' replied Jake, smiling sarcastically at him.

'Some host you are,' replied Ben, as he, too, tried to steal one of Jake's crisps.

Twenty minutes or so later, both of the TSG guys joined Jake and Ted at the house.

'What's for dinner, Sarge?' asked one of the team.

'Whatever you want to cook yourself,' said both Jake and Ben, chuckling.

CHAPTER 8

Outside M&S, Oxford Street

By the time Ted arrived at the M&S murder scene, the statement hungry, 'sell-my-granny for a story' reporters, apparently representing every rag-tag newspaper and TV news channel in the country had gathered and were in full-swing snapping mode. Ted pushed his way through the swarm, and spoke to one of the uniformed inspectors who seemed to be in charge.

'Why the fuck is that man still dangling down the side of the fucking building?' Ted asked angrily.

'The area directly in front of the rail he is hanging from seems to have a pressure pad of some sort preventing anyone getting anywhere near it. We're waiting for the bomb disposal guys to give us the all clear,' replied the inspector.

'Have you guys never heard of the fucking fire brigade? They have big, big ladders that can reach him from the other fucking side of the building.' Ted retorted angrily.

'They're on the way, Sir,' replied the softly spoken and highly embarrassed Inspector.

'In the meantime, get some crowd control organised,' Ted ordered impatiently, before making his way into the building.

Once on the roof, Ted saw a few familiar faces, one of which was the Army Bomb Disposal Unit captain who had attended the Ben Hickson and Annie cases. Ted knew from past experience that the young captain liked to think he was in control in these situations. He was not one to be messed with. So, Ted simply waited on the other side of the roof, whilst the captain dealt with whatever it doing.

A few minutes later, the captain lifted up the so-called pressure pad and declared it a hoax.

Ted made his way to the Army Captain. 'Well, what was it'? he asked.

'Basically, it was a large door-mat with a couple of old newspapers stuffed under it and a few loose wires. 'Completely harmless and a waste of my time.' grumbled the captain, as he began to remove his armoured protective equipment. Ted, ignoring the
captain's whinging, took over the crime scene.
He pointed to a number of uniformed officers. 'You, you and you, get that body up and be careful not to decapitate it in the process,' he barked.
Leaving them to get on with it, Ted carried out a quick survey of the building's roof top, then left the scene to make his way to the Royal Free Hospital where the badly injured security guard, Kean's colleague, was being treated.

Sgt. Pete Machin was having a little doze in the car when Ted got in.
'Sorry boss, I was up all night with our Jenny. She's having a real hard time of it just lately. It's getting

harder and harder to deal with her the older she gets,' Pete apologised.

'No need to apologise to me, Pete. Take me to the Royal Free, will you?' Ted told him.

'Wilko,' replied Pete, as he started the car.

After interviewing the second security guard, who said he hadn't seen his attacker, and could not offer any useful information. Frustrated, Ted pulled out his mobile and called Bob Griffiths, the Yard's press liaison officer.

'Bob, it's Ted. I want you to give a press conference and announce the discovery of the second security guard. It may well draw this Alex character out if he knows there's a potential witness that may be able to identify him.'

'Is that wise, Ted? You'll be putting the guard at risk, and we both know that Alex Langdon is a very capable killer,' Bob said, with an air of caution.

'Don't worry about this chap. I'll double up the security. It's important that we draw Alex out into the open, put a spanner in the works, so to speak,'

Ted was saying, when he was interrupted by the alarms starting up. Nurses and doctors rushed into the

security guard's room.

'What's all that racket about?' asked Bob.

'I'll get back to you in a few minutes, Bob,' said Ted, rapidly hanging up the call and rushing into the private room where the injured guard was receiving CPR. Within five minutes, the medics declared the him

dead.

Ted called Bob Back on his mobile. 'Bob, it's me again. The security guard has just died, but I still want

that press conference to go ahead. Just leave out the bit about him dying. Oh, and also, you might drop a subtle hint as to which hospital he's at.' he added.

'Okay, Ted, I can do that. But I don't think Tingy will be happy about the fact that we're not declaring the guard's death,'

'Fuck Tingy. And, as far as protecting your ass, this conversation didn't take place,' said Ted, cutting the call and pocketing his phone.

From his vantage point outside the hospital, Alex watched on, easily spotting Ted as he eventually left the hospital. Alex had followed the detective there from the M&S murder scene. He was curious as to why Ted had gone from the crime scene straight to the hospital. It certainly wasn't to visit David Kean; he was well and truly dead. But maybe he'd been sloppy with the other security guard? Alex thought about it for a few minutes and concluded that it was of no consequence. The guard had almost certainly not seen

his face, as he'd attacked him from behind.

He started up his car, and followed Ted from a distance in his unmarked vehicle.

CHAPTER 9

The Safehouse

Twenty minutes later, Ted's car pulled up on the drive of a detached house in Beverley Gardens, Golders Green. Alex watched as the door to the property was opened by a uniformed cop holding a G36C assault

rifle.

TSG? Now that is interesting. I wonder who's being protected here? He grabbed his rifle sight to take a closer look. 'You beauty,' he murmured to himself, as he scanned the upstairs bedroom window and caught

a glimpse of his old friend Ben Hickson.

Once inside the house, Ted invited Ben and Carole to join him for a coffee in the kitchen.

'I'm sure you've been made aware of the fact that our old friend Alex Langdon is back in town.

What you probably don't know is that he has only been back in the country for three days and has already brutally killed two people. He has indicated via a note found at his latest murder scene that his intention is to finish the job on you. I also believe that I may also be a target, for having saved you last time. Hence, the reason you're going to be staying put here, with this very good protection team until we have him in custody, or he's dead. For real, this time,' said Ted,

looking directly at Ben.

'How can you be sure that I'll be safe here? If I know Alex, it won't take him long to work out where you're keeping me.' said a visibly nervous Ben.

'We're organising another safehouse location and we'll be moving you there as soon as all the security measures are in place. A few days or so tops, promise.' Ted reassured him.

'The sooner the better,' said Ben, reaching for the comfort of the biscuit barrel.

'Well, if there is nothing else, I need to go and catch this psycho.' Said Ted, swallowing the last dregs of his coffee.

'Can I have a word with you in private, Sir?' asked Carole.

'Sir, I don't want to come across as a whinger, but would I be better employed actively looking for our killer, rather than baby-sitting our man in there?' she asked, as they stood in the hallway.

'Your job, Detective Sergeant, is to do as directed. At this moment in time I have directed that you 'babysit', which, by the way, is a very important role. As long as our man in there is alive, Alex Langdon will continue to look for him and remain in this country. That gives us a better chance of catching him. However, if you're not up to the job, I could always ask Tingy to reassign you…' Ted said, pointing in the direction of the kitchen and not looking too pleased about his new partner questioning his decision.

'Sorry, Sir, and I assure you I'm more that up to it,' said Carole, clearly feeling well and truly put in her place.

CHAPTER 10

The Stakeout

After observing the house at Beverley Gardens, Alex had gained a fairly good understanding of the potential hazards that lay in store for him, if and when he was to snatch Ben. He could have just stormed the house, or even blown it up. But that wouldn't be spectacular enough, he thought. Plus, he wanted to see

the look on Ben's face as he killed him.

Alex waited for Ted and his colleague to leave before taking a walk around the backs of the houses opposite the safehouse. After twenty minutes, he felt he'd gathered sufficient intel, and returned to the Hilton, stopping off at a local hardware store on the way.

Back in his room, Alex ordered room service of steak and chips and set about preparing his plan, followed by a nap.

At eight in the evening, the alarm on Alex's clock woke him from the usual disturbing dreams. Having thrown the radio-alarm clock across the room, Alex got up and took a cold shower before getting
dressed.

Forty minutes later, Alex, carrying two boxes containing 16″ Domino pizzas in one hand and his 9mm pistol in the other, knocked on the door of number 16 Beverley Gardens. The hallway light came
on and a voice from inside asked.

'Who's there?' asked a male voice.

'Pizza delivery,' called out Alex.

'What?... We haven't ordered any pizzas. Go away please.'

   'I'm sorry, Sir, but I have two pizzas for number 16 Beverley Gardens,' Alex politely replied.

'Hold on,' said the voice from inside, as Alex heard the occupant taking off the chain and unbolting the door.

'I've to…'the elderly male at the door started to say as he opened it., but was cut off, as Alex pushed into the house. The old man fell to the floor, scrambling for his glasses, which had fallen off. Glasses recovered; the old man now found himself looking down the barrel of Alex's 9mm pistol.

'Not a word, or I'll kill you both. Do I make myself clear?' Alex tapped the old man's head with the barrel of the pistol.

'Call your wife and tell her to come here,' ordered Alex.

'She's not my wife, she's my sister,' mumbled the old man.

'I don't give a shit what relation she is to you. Just get the bitch here,' bellowed Alex, tapping the old man, with the pistol again.

The old man raised his arms to his head protectively.

'Okay, okay, I'll do it. Cath,' called the old man, 'come here please, and quickly.'

'Whatever is it, Sydney, you know I'm' The old lady entered the hall and stopped in her tracks as she saw Alex standing over her brother, aiming a gun at his head.

'Come here and kneel next to Sydney,' Alex ordered her.

The old lady quickly complied, and Alex hog tied the pair before bungling them down the cellar stairs and locking the door. Then he went upstairs and set up his observation point in the front upstairs bedroom.

Alex was watching through the upstairs window, when he saw a black BMW pull on to the drive of the safehouse. There were two occupants in the car, one of whom made a phone call on his mobile before both men emerged from the car and made their way to the door.

Both wore longish trench coats, and carried what Alex knew to be weapon transportation bags, known in the trade as WTBs. As the pair reached the front door, it was opened from the inside.

Ten minutes later, two different guys left the house and drove off in the BMW. Again, both carried WTBs Alex made a note of the time, 22.00 hours.

At 22.30 hours, Alex noticed a figure coming from the back of the house carrying black waste sack, which he deposited in the bin to the side of the property.

Alex knew from his time at the Yard, that both surveillance and protection shifts usually changed over on a four-six hourly rota. So, he decided to make himself a coffee, and find something to eat.

Three and a half hours later, Alex was back at his observation point in the front bedroom of number 16. He knew it might be another two and half hours before there was going to be any movement across the road. *But there are always the keen ones that like to arrive early*, he thought to himself. His hunch was right. He smiles, as the same black BMW as before pulled on to the drive at 01:40 hours, a good twenty minutes before the end

of the shift.

Once again, one of the two occupants made a phone call, before the two of them carrying their WTBs entered the house. As before, ten minutes later two other men drove off in the BMW.

So, it's four-hour shifts, is it? Alex thought, using the information to calculate the best time to attack. He knew the streets might be too populated during the next changeover at 06:00 hours, which could hamper his getaway. Instead, he opted to wait it out until 02:00 hours the following day.

Knowing that there would likely be no action for the next few hours, Alex set an alarm on his mobile for 05:30 hours, and took a nap.

CHAPTER 11

Preparation Prevents Piss-Poor Performance.

The alarm on Alex's phone rang just in time. Alex had been dreaming. *Once again, he found himself wearing a bright orange jumpsuit. This time, though, he was trapped in a metal cage that was suspended in the air. Below the cage was a pyramid of wood. He looked at the crowd of about sixty people who had gathered below for wat he knew was one purpose – to punish the infidel. Alex noticed a lone figure holding a blazing touch. The face was covered, but Alex could see the eyes of the lone figure, they were bright blue, definitely not the eyes of a middle eastern, Alex thought. The blue-eyed figure stepped forward, torch held high, then pulled down its mask. It was the face of Annie Harris. She smiled at Alex, as she leaned forward to light the pyramid of timber stacked below his prison…*

Alex jerked awake, heart pounding and suddenly feeling exhausted. Nevertheless, he forced himself onto his feet, and took up his position at the bedroom window. As he waited for the 06.00 hours change over, he thought about the dream he'd just had. The nightmares were definitely getting more frequent and a lot eerier. *Maybe I really am going mad,* he wondered, his eyes fixed on the house opposite.

At 05.55 hours, the BMW once again rolled on to the drive, and Alex observed the same proceedings as the before, as the changeover took place.

Changeover complete, Ted decided to take a shower, then went to the kitchen. He was hungry and hoped the Old Gets had something decent to eat. The fridge, though, was almost empty. All he could find was a few salad vegetables, a tub of butter and a pack of bacon. Luckily there was also a loaf of bread in the breadbin.

Once he had eaten his bacon sarnie and drunk his coffee, he went down to the cellar to check on his hosts. As he turned the cellar light on, he could see the old man lying motionless on the floor. He had dried blood which seem to have come from his ear and the underside was showing signs of lividity, a sure sign that the old man was dead.

His sister was kneeling next to him crying and rocking back and forth, whilst whimpering through her gag.

Alex lowered her gag.

'You've killed him, you've killed my Sydney you bastard,' the old lady screamed, before spitting in Alex's face.

With one punch Alex knocked her out cold, then wiped the spit off his face. Alex couldn't stand people spitting at him. It always brought back memories of being in captivity. Where, every time one of his captors said something, each sentence would end with them spitting at him. Alex lifted the old lady's limp head and slashed her throat.

Why did you have to do that? I was going to let you both live. He looked back at the two dead OAPs, before closing the cellar door and returning to the kitchen to plan his attack.

Luckily for Alex, the house opposite and the one he was currently occupying were identical as far as layout was concerned. This made Alex's job a lot easier. All he had to do was prepare his weapons. He knew from his time as a close protection specialist with the SAS and Valha that the best time to attack was within the first ten minutes of a changeover, the new guards would have to familiarise themselves with their new surroundings, and usually one of them would end up making a brew. Whilst the other would brief Ben on the action plan and escape route should they be attacked.

CHAPTER 12

Re-deployment

Ted sat in his office drinking his fifth coffee of the day. This mornings' hangover was probably one of the worst he'd had in a while. He took another couple of paracetamols and opened the Alex Langdon file. *Why is it so difficult to catch this creep*, he wondered to himself? *Surely, he isn't that good?* Deep in thought, Ted stared at the picture of the four SAS guys he had liberated from Ben's pub, which now hung on his office wall.

The next few photos pinned up there were of Annie's murder scene. Ted still couldn't understand why Alex had been so cruel to her, especially since she had once been his lover.

The phone rang.

'Ted Baxter.' he answered.

'Ah, Ted, it's Max. There have been a few developments. I want you to come to my office pronto, and bring the Alex Langdon file with you.''

'Give me five minutes' replied Ted, wondering what the 'developments' might be.

Minutes later, Ted knocked on the chief-super's door.

'Enter,' said a voice from inside.

'Fucking enter? Who does he think he is, the headmaster?' thought Ted, entering the office.

'You asked to see me, Boss.'

'Yes, Ted. As I said, there have been a few developments. Sit down, will you?' Max gestured at the two chairs positioned in front of his desk and waited for Ted to settle before continuing. 'Firstly, the anti-terrorist squad are carrying out a number of raids around the country. Birmingham, Leicester Manchester, etcetera. As a result, they've requisitioned most of the TSG guys for a few days.

'Meaning?' questioned Ted.

'Meaning, Chief Inspector, you will have to reduce the number of TSG guys guarding Ben Hickson.'

'I can't reduce the number of guys, Sir. Standard operating procedure states that there must be at least two TSG guards, plus one of us,'

'I don't need you to remind me of the SOP's, thank you, Chief. You'll have to double their shifts.

You'll only have six TSG at your disposal, so they'll have to do eight hours on and sixteen off for the next few days. Starting with the team that takes over at 10am this morning,' barked Max.

'Is that all, Sir?'

'No, actually it isn't,' said Max, picking up the phone. 'Rachel, can you ask Chief Inspector Allocco to step into my office, please?' He replaced the receiver.

A few seconds later, the Italian detective entered.

'Chief Inspector Allocco, I'd like you to meet Chief Baxter,' Max said, gesturing for the pair to shake hands and for Allocco to sit.

'Ted, as you are aware, our man Alex Langdon, has recently taken a trip over the water, and, while he was there, committed some horrific crimes, none more so than those he committed in Turin. As a result of these heinous crimes, the Italian police commissioner is keen to help capture Alex Langdon, and has offered us help in the form of Chief Allocco here. He pointed to Antonio. He is, I have it on good authority, one of the very best investigators in the Italian Police.' Allocco smiled modestly, as Max continued. 'The commissioners on both sides want you and Chief Allocco to work together in the hunt and apprehension of Langdon.'

'I already have a partner,' Ted said.

'I've re-deployed her for the time being. Chief Allocco will be your partner until Langdon is caught or dead. Understood, Chief Inspector?'

Reluctantly, Ted agreed. *I'll just bung him on baby-sitting duty and keep him out of my hair*, he thought to himself.

'Now, Chief Allocco, would you mind stepping out of the office for a minute or two, whilst I discuss anther matter with Chief Baxter?' said Max, waving his hand in the direction of the door.

Once Allocco had shut the door, Max said, 'Now Ted, I know you're probably not too keen to have this Italian fellow shadowing you, but he is one of the very best. He's got a reputation second to none, present company excepted, of course.' Ted forced a smile at the compliment. 'So, I want you to treat him with the highest respect. Which means don't just dump him in the safe house or leave him dangling around in your office. Understood?' Max looked at Ted warningly.

'Understood, Boss,' replied Ted, mentally tipping his non-existent hat, before leaving.

'Follow me, Chief Inspector Allocco,' he said, finding the Italian waiting outside, and leading the way to his own office.

'Please, call me Antonio,' replied Allocco.

Alex ignored the request, and stopped off at the coffee machine in the hallway.

'Want one?' Ted asked.

'No, thank you, I have my own,' said Allocco, smiling as he pointed the leather holdall he was carrying.

Once back in his office, Ted cleared a space on what was once Annie's desk.

'There you go, make yourself at home,' he said.

'Thank you, I will,' replied Allocco, as he unzipped his leather holdall.

Ted waited patiently and watched on as the little Italian policeman unpacked his coffee machine, filled it with bottled water and made himself a perfect expresso. The fragrance filled the room, as the pair sat down to swap case files with each other.

'Our man Alex Langdon is one nasty piece of work!' Allocco concluded, when they finally closed each other's files.

'Indeed. I think it's about time you meet Ben Hickson, the guy that started all of this,' Ted said, picking up the phone and asking Pete Machin to bring a car around to the front of the building.

Forty minutes later, Ted was introducing Chief Allocco to Ben Hickson.

'So, you served with this man Alex Langdon. You must have a good understanding of how he operates,' said Allocco, as he peered through a tiny gap in the blind of the front ground floor window.

'I know he's a fucking psycho who will stop at nothing. His nickname in the SAS was Natural, as in Natural Born Killer. He really gets off on killing people. He used to say that he loved the taste he got in his mouth as he killed,' replied Ben.

'Ah, the metallic taste of blood. I have once tasted it myself. A horrible taste, 'said Allocco, still peering through the gap in the blind.

Ben looked at Ted, and pointed to Allocco, as if to say is he for real? Ted held his hands out palms up and shrugged his shoulders to indicate that he had no clue.

'Can you see something out there, Chief Allocco?' asked Ted, curious to know what the Italian found so interesting.

'No. I am just amused at the amount of curtain twitching going on out there. You Brits certainly are nosy,' replied Allocco, as he turned to face them smiling like the Cheshire Cat.

'As I said, Mr Hickson, we'll be moving you to a more secluded location tomorrow morning at 10am. You'll be safe here until then,' said Ted.

CHAPTER 13

Beverley Gardens

When Ted's unmarked police car pulled on to the drive of the safe house at 10.20am, Alex was at his observation position. He had been at the upstairs window of number 16, waiting for the 10am TSG change over, which still hadn't happened.

Alex recognised two of the three guys who exited the car. The other one was familiar, but Alex couldn't quite put a name to the face?

As he watched them step inside, Alex wondered why the TSG changeover pattern had changed. Twenty minutes or so later, he was still watching when the three men emerged from the house. He picked up his rifle sight and took a closer look at the third unknown man. As he did so, the little guy looked straight up in the direction of the window Alex was sitting at.

Ted noticed that the little detective had something on his mind. 'Is there something on your mind, Chief Allocco?'

'No, no, Chief Baxter, I was merely contemplating why English people have such an obsession about complete privacy to the extent that they would hide themselves behind such horrible net curtains. So old fashioned, do you not think, Chief?'

'I can't say I've noticed, nor care,' said Ted, getting into the front seat and pulling his seatbelt across his chest.

Alex stepped back away from the window. Not that he needed to, there was no chance the stranger could have seen him through the old-fashioned, nicotine-stained net curtains that hung over the window.

Alex watched on as the little guy scratched his head thoughtfully, before joining the other two in the car.

Go it! He suddenly remembered where he'd seen the guy before. It was the Italian equivalent of Ted Baxter, the one who had been in charge of the Maniceni case back in Turin. Alex remembered seeing him at the Maniceni's house.

Chief Inspector Allocco, or something like that. Scotland Yard must really be desperate, if they have called on the Italians for help.

Knowing that he had at least four hours to spare before the next possible change over, Alex decided to use the time to shower and prepare a breakfast of bacon and eggs. After which, he stopped off at a local hardware store, then visited one of his old underworld supply contacts.

CHAPTER 14

Alex's old flat on Sloan Street

After visiting Ben at the safehouse, Chief Allocco requested that Ted take him to Alex's old apartment. Allocco felt that a visit to the killer's lair might allow him to gain greater understanding of how Alex Langdon ticked.

Having nothing to go on as yet, Ted agreed, and they drove to Langdon's apartment on Sloan Street.

'Right, Sergeant, open it up,' Ted told Sergeant Machin, when they stood at the door of the apartment.

'I don't think you're going to find out anything about our boy you don't already know, Chief Allocco,' said Ted, as he waved the Italian ahead of him into the apartment.

'You are probably right, Chief Inspector Baxter, but I don't see any harm in trying, do you?' replied Allocco, entering the apartment.

Allocco stood and slowly looked around the large lounge in his usual silent manner, stopping occasionally to scratch his head. Ted and Sergeant Machin studied the Italian's peculiar mannerisms.

'I told you there was probably nothing to see,' said Ted, getting a little impatient.

Allocco ignored him and carried on surveying a row of framed photos on a shelf. He held one up and pointed at it, as if asking a question. Ted knew what he was about to ask.

'Yes, it's Annie Harris, my former colleague and, unfortunately, that scumbag's former girlfriend,' said Ted, dismissively.

Allocco picked up another photo, this one was of Alex Langdon dressed up in country shooting attire, tweed jacket and flat cap, wellies and a gilet. He was holding a broken shotgun under one arm and a brace of pheasant in the other.

Allocco scratched his head once more, as he scrutinized the photo.

'Now, Chief Baxter, this is interesting,' said Allocco, showing the photo to Ted.

'It's just a hunting picture,' said Ted. 'Everyone has their picture taken with their shoot at the end of the day's grouse shoot. Obviously, our man likes to go shooting. Nothing strange about that.'

'Look a little closer, Chief Baxter. This man looks very at home in this picture. And also, look at the driveway. There are no cars, which would suggest that this wasn't an organised shoot, and that this picture was taken at his own property, maybe?? Ted peered at the photo.

Allocco then produced a magnifying glass from his jacket inside pocket. 'Oak Orchard Hall,' he read. 'Could this be another property that he may own, and possibly the place where he may be hiding?'

Ted took the photo from Allocco. 'Maybe,' replied Ted, thinking *Fuck, why didn't we spot that*

He took out his mobile phone and rang Danny.

'Hey, Ted, what's up?'

'Danny, I want you to get in touch with the land registry office and check out who owns Oak Orchard Hall in Gloucester. I want the answer by the time I get back to the yard, 'ordered Ted.

'Will do, Ted. Is it to do with the Alex Langdon case?' Danny asked.

'Yes, and it's urgent,' said Ted, hanging up.

Ted took the photo from Chief Allocco, as well as the one of Alex and Annie, before leaving the apartment to return to the Yard.

By the time they got back, Danny had already received word from the land registry, and was waiting in Ted's office.

'Hi, Ted' said Danny said, as he jumped out of Ted's chair.

'Relax, Danny,' Ted said, waving him back down into the chair.

'I've got the feedback from the land registry. The registered owner of the property is indeed Mike Travis.' Danny reported.

'Okay, thanks. I need you to call the local bobbies.'

'I hope you don't mind, Ted, but I've already called the Gloucester constabulary and they're sending someone over there as we speak. I've given them your mobile number and asked them to contact you directly.'

'Excellent work, Danny. You're definitely getting the hang of this detective lark. You should consider transferring,' said Ted, pleased with his new prodigy.

'Anyone for one the Yard's finest heart attacks on a plate?' Ted asked.

Allocco picked up his little leather bag.

'I know, you've brought your own,' Ted said, before the Italian could speak.

'Looks like it's just me and thee, Danny-Boy, said Ted, as he guided young Danny through the office door.

'I'll see you in twenty minutes or so, Chief Allocco.'

Ted and Danny were tucking into their breakfast when Ted's mobile started to vibrate across the table.

'Hello, Ted Baxter here.'

'Is that Chief Inspector Baxter?' asked a female voice.

'Yes,' replied Ted, slightly annoyed. He could never get his head around people's obsession of confirming his name despite having called him.

'It's Inspector Flowers from Gloucester CID here. I'm calling in response to your request that we visit Oak Orchard Hall.'

'Oh, yes?'

'We sent a couple of our local bobbies around to the house, as requested. It seems to have been unoccupied for quite some time. However, there was a horrible stench around the house, and on further investigation the officers located the source of the smell. It was coming from several corpses that had been buried under the floor of the orangery, six in all. 'We've set up a cordon around the estate, and I have my SOCCOs en-route. I take it you can shed some light on the situation, Chief Inspector?'

'Don't let anyone near the crime scene until I arrive. I'll be with you as soon as I can,' said Ted, hanging up and pushing the plate of half-eaten food aside.

'Right, I think a trip to Gloucester is in order. Danny get hold of Pete Machin. We'll meet you out front,' he said.

'Will do, Boss.'

'Am I invited along, too, Chief Inspector?' asked Allocco.

'Yes, of course, and please, call me Ted.

CHAPTER 15

Beverly Gardens

Alex watched on as the fresh pair of TSG cops rolled up in the now familiar black BMW. Alex checked his watch. 13.50 hours. *So, now we know they're on eight-hour shifts. That makes life a bit easier*, Alex thought to himself, as he watched the two guys enter the house across the way.

A few minutes after the other two TSG cops had left, Alex himself exited the rear of number 16. He needed some extra rations and a few tools for later.

His first stop was a hardware store, where he purchased some heavy-duty bin liners, some chain link and a glass cutter.

He next stopped off to visit one of his old suppliers, where he purchased half a kilo of plastic explosive and several boxes of 9mm ammunition, plus a silencer for his Browning. Finally, he stopped off at a Londis convenience store to buy some food.

On his return to number 16, Alex securely wrapped the bodies of Cath and Sydney with the plastic bin sacks. *It must be an age thing*, he thought to himself, as he worked. *Older dead people always seem to decompose quicker than the younger ones.* He rolled the bodies into the far corner of the cellar. He then turned his attention to the house's alarm system, which was housed down there.

Once he had sorted out the two old codgers and the alarm, Alex made himself a meal of steak and salad. He sat down to eat, and turned on the television. The five o'clock news was just starting.

'Good afternoon,' announced the news reader. 'In breaking news, Police say that they have discovered several bodies at a manor house in Gloucester. Police say the badly composed bodies were found buried under the floor of the orangery adjoining the house. So far, they have discovered six bodies in total. However, the search for more bodies is continuing.' A shot of a helicopter above his, or rather Mike Travis's, old house appeared on screen. Alex turned the TV off. He didn't need the news to tell him who was buried there. After all, he was the one who had put them there.

After eating, Alex took up his position at his observation point in the upstairs front bedroom. As expected, another TSG changeover took place between 17.50 and 18.10 hours. *Great, the next changeover will be at 02.00 hours. That means I can get a few hours kip,* he thought with satisfaction.

CHAPTER 16

The end of a long day

It was half-past-nine by the time Ted had dropped Antonio Allocco off at the Hotel Paradise, a three-star, back street hovel that only tourists who were clueless to its reputation as a part time brothel and the Met's visiting guests stayed. Ted remembered turning the place over on many occasions, back in his uniformed days.

Having dismissed the driver at the Paradise, he walked home to his bedsit, first calling at an off-licence to pick up a bottle of vodka and a fast-food joint for a Chinese takeaway.

Tucking into his special chop-suey, Ted contemplated his day. *It's certainly been an eventful day,* he thought. *Firs, having to convince Cruella Monk of his fitness to return to duty, then meeting the quirky little Italian and him spotting that picture of Alex's other house, and as a result, discovering the six bodies buried under the orangery. I need a bit of you,* he thought, reaching for the vodka and unscrewing the cap before pouring himself a long one. He then turned his attention to his chicken chop suey.

After he had finished his meal, Ted took out the picture of Alex and Annie that he' liberated from Alex's apartment earlier. He looked at it for several seconds, then angrily tore away the part of the photo containing Alex's image, which he threw in the waste bin. He then stared the image of Annie, fantasising about what he would do to that cocksucker Alex when and if he eventually got his hands on him. Ted hoped that when that moment came, there would just be the two of them, and Ted would show no mercy as he avenged Annie's murder.

He poured himself another drink and downed it in one, before sinking his tired body into the sofa bed, where he promptly fell asleep.

Back at Beverley Gardens, Alex's phone alarm went off. Normally, the sound of the alarm would annoy him, but this time he was grateful for the interruption – once again he'd been having a distressing nightmare. This time he was being chased by the skeletons of all of his victims. They were all still wearing the same clothes they'd been wearing when he'd killed them. There was Annie in her underwear with no head, Pete-the-Print in his flat cap and Barbour jacket, and Mike's old nanny in her crochet shawl. Surprisingly, the old nanny was the fastest of them all. She'd almost caught up with him. Still sweating profusely, he eventually rolled himself of bed and went to the bathroom to take a cold shower, before heading to the kitchen to make himself a coffee and a snack.

Following his meal, he spent the next ninety minutes preparing his tools and mentally running through his plan of attack. Eventually, he dressed for the occasion all in black. As he looked at himself in the bedroom's full-length mirror, he recalled a time when he last wore such an outfit. As an SAS trooper, he was frequently required to be part of the SAS's antiterrorist team. That was usually a squadron of men whose job it was to attend terrorist incidents that might occur in the UK, such as the Iranian Embassy siege.

He had never been involved in an actual homeland operation, but he had practiced virtually every possible scenario, from freeing hostages held in in various buildings to storming a hijacked plane.

Once dressed, Alex took up his position at the bedroom window and waited for the 2am changeover at the house opposite. As he sat peering through his binoculars, Alex already had a hint of the taste of killing in his mouth.

Finally, at 01.50 hours, the now familiar black BMW rolled onto the drive of the safe house. Alex watched while the changeover took place.

Once the out-going pair of men had left Alex, gathered his equipment and made his way across the road and into the rear garden of the house next door to that of the safe house. From his new position, through his binoculars, Alex could observe his prey. He could see through the kitchen window of the safe house that one of the TSG was sitting at the kitchen table, working on a laptop. Alex assumed that Ben would be asleep at this hour of the morning, and that the other TSG officer was probably at the front of the house.

After about ten minutes, Alex saw the bathroom light come on. *Now is the time to strike, h*e told himself, then climbed stealthily over the fence separating the two gardens. Pausing in the shadows of the safe house garden, he reached into his pocket and took out his mobile phone, entered a code, pressed send and instantly heard with satisfaction the house alarm at number 16 across the road go off.

Alex watched through the window, as the TSG officer jumped up from the kitchen table and ran through to the front of the house.

Once he was out of sight, Alex quickly kicked in the back door, and ran through the kitchen, shooting the officer stone dead. He then ran up the stairs just in time to catch the other officer coming out of the loo still trying to do up his trousers. Again, with one well aimed shot, the TSG officer went down like a lead balloon.

Ben, woken by the house alarm quickly followed by the sound of the back door being kicked in, didn't hang around. He climbed through the bedroom window

and dropped onto the porchway roof below, before legging it down the road and narrowly avoiding being hit by an oncoming car.

Alex searched the rest of the house for Ben in vain.

CHAPTER 17

Dream date with Annie

It was 1.00am when Ted woke up on the sofa. His clothes were wringing wet with sweat and his heart was beating through his chest. He had been having a rather distressing nightmare about Annie.

He dreamt that Annie was still alive and that he had finally plucked up the courage to ask her on a date. She accepted and they agreed to meet at the Dorchester Grill at 7pm.

When Ted arrived at the Dorchester, the waiter informed him that his guest (Annie) had changed the booking slightly, and they would now be dining in one of the Dorchester's private dining rooms.

The waiter took him to the door of the private dining room and indicated that Ted should enter.

Ted opened the door. As he put his head around the door, he saw Anni sitting at a table dressed in just her underwear. Around her neck she was wearing some kind of collar, which had a cord attached to it. She was also gagged.

Ted instantly ran toward her. As he did so, her heard a distinct click that seemed to come from something hidden under the Persian rug.

Thinking that it was a pressure switch, Ted stood frozen to the spot. Bollocks, what do I do now? he thought franticly. He reached into his pocket for his mobile, intending to call Jake and have him get the bomb disposal guys. But it wasn't a pressure switch he was standing on, as he soon discovered. It was a timer switch that, just as he began to call Jake, went off and blew Annie's head off. Again.

Ted poured himself a large vodka and downed it in one. He then stripped from his sweat soaked clothes and took a shower.

Whilst in the shower, Ted thought about his future with the Met. He knew that the job was getting harder, and he was increasingly relying on the vodka to get through. *That's never a good thing*, he thought, deciding that Alex Langdon would be his last case. Once the scumbag was either dead or locked up for life, Ted would retire to the south coast.

Finished with his shower, Ted unfolded the sofa bed, something he hadn't ever done since moving into the bedsit eight months ago. He then attempted to get some more sleep.

After twenty uncomfortable minutes of tossing and turning on the sofa bed's paper-thin-mattress, he gave up trying to sleep and telephoned the Yard to order a car to pick him up and take him to the safe house.

May as well see if our man Ben can identify any of the bodies that were found at Oak Orchard Hal, Ted thought to himself, while he hunted for a cleanish shirt and waited for the car to arrive.

Ted sat in the back seat of the car reviewing the photos of the Oak Orchard Hall victims, when he was suddenly thrown from one side of the car to the other. The driver had swerved and braked sharply to avoid someone who had run in front of the car.

'What the fuck!' the driver exclaimed, as both he and Ted watched the individual run off down the street.

'Shit,' said Ted, recognising the figure they had nearly just run over. 'It's bloody Ben Hickson! Stop the car,' he barked.

As the car came to a halt, Ted jumped out. 'Go after him,' he told the driver. 'I'm going to the house,' he added, legging it toward the safe house.

Ted approached the house cautiously. He tried the front door. It was locked. He made his way quietly to the rear of the property, where he saw that the back door had been kicked in. *Bollock, bollocks and more bollocks,* he thought, cautiously entering the eerily quiet and dark house. As he made his way to the hallway, he found one of the TSG officers laid on the floor. He knelt down to check for a pulse, but it was absent. Ted picked up the dead officer's G36C assault rifle, and proceeded nervously to search the house.

The downstairs was clear, so Ted carefully crept up the stairs. The third step creaked loudly when Ted placed his size ten brogue upon it. He grimaced, and continued stealthily to the top of the stairs, where he spotted a second TSG office lying next to the bathroom door. Again, Ted knelt to check for a pulse. As bent down, something struck him on the back of the head, and he fell into blackness.

Alex was searching the upstairs rooms of the house, when he heard the sound of a weapon being cocked and footsteps on the creaking stairs. He hid behind the bedroom door, peering through the gap. It was Ted Baxter. Alex waited for Ted to bend down to check on the TSG officer, then hit him over the head with his 9mm Browning.

As Alex continued to search the house for Ben, he heard a car pull up on the drive. He looked through the window to see that the car had a single occupant. *Probably Ted's driver? Probably unarmed?* Alex made his way to the downstairs hallway.

He stood in complete darkness at the bottom of the stairs, waiting for the silhouette of the cop to appear at the back door. As he waited, he could feel his heart pounding frantically in his chest, and the now very familiar and pleasurable metallic taste of killing engulfed his mouth. *It reminds me of my time in the SAS, sitting in some bush or in a shell-scrape, waiting for the enemy to appear.*

The silhouette appeared at the back door. A second later the body of the cop fell to the floor. Alex's well-aimed shot penetrated the coppers right eye socket and continued on. It went straight through his brain and out of the back of his neck. The youngish policeman lay crumpled on the floor. It reminded Alex of Stan Buxton, and the way his body had dropped like a sack of spuds once both of his arms, which were holding his legless body, were simultaneously blown off.

After removing the car keys from the dead police driver's pocket, Alex made his way back up the stairs, where he tied Ted Baxter's hands and feet and gagged him, before dragging his limp body down the stairs and into the boot of the unmarked police car. Alex next drove the car around to the back of number 16 and parked it in the garage.

Once in the garage and hidden from the sight of prying eyes, Alex opened the car's boot and injected the still unconscious Ted with a syringe full of scopolamine. *There, that should keep you quiet for a few hours,* Alex thought, as he removed Ted's mobile phone from his jacket pocket before closing the boot and making his way to his own car, which was parked down the road.

Once in his car, Alex drove over to his old apartment block's underground car park, where he hid Ted's mobile in the roof of the elevator. Then, he returned to number sixteen.

Once inside, Alex once more took up his observation position in the front bedroom. Pissed off about the fact that that he had once again failed to deal with the disloyal scumbag Ben, he contemplated what to do with Supercop Ted Baxter. *Should I just kill him and dump his body in the cellar with the old codgers, or should I execute him Alex style, publicly? I'll have to give it some thought.* He scanned the safe house over the road through the net curtain.

Having secured the house before leaving, he was not expecting the bodies of the three dead cops to be discovered until 10.00 hours the following morning, when the next changeover was due to take place. This provided Alex the opportunity to get some much-needed rest. He set the alarm on his phone for 06.00 hours, before laying down on the bed and drifting off to sleep.

CHAPTER 18

The Paradise Hotel, 06.00 hours Antonio Allocco sat on the end of his hotel bed. He hadn't slept very much at all. The occupants of the rooms above, below and to the side of his seemed to be having very loud sex all night.

Having decided enough was enough, Allocco decided to take a shower and then go to find a café, and maybe treat himself to an infamous Full English breakfast before making his way to Scotland Yard. Not that he had a clue where Scotland yard was.

He didn't have to walk far before he came across Gunter's Café. According to the banner that stretched across the café window, which claimed that they served the best English breakfast in London.

Allocco contemplated the sign, finding it somewhat ironic that the best English breakfast in London was actually cooked by someone with a German name.

As he entered the café, the smell of greasy food overwhelmed his sense of smell. He looked about the empty café, which at least seemed clean. As he took a seat near the window, a small, scruffy woman wearing a grease-spotted pink apron appeared from behind the counter.

'Good morning,' said the woman, who smiled and exposed her lack of several upper and lower teeth. The ones she did have were pretty rotten, too.

'Good morning, Madam,' replied Allocco, now wishing he hadn't sat down.

'What can I get you, darlin?' The woman asked with a cockney accent, exposing her lack of teeth once again.

Hesitantly, Allocco ordered an English breakfast and a coffee.

'Do you want milk and sugar in ya coffee?'

'Black, please.'

'Fried or toast?'

Allocco looked confused.

'Do you want fried bread or toast with your breakfast?' she explained, transferring her weight from one foot to the other.

'Toast, please.'

'Tomatoes or beans?'

'Tomatoes,' replied Allocco, who was getting a little bit tired of hearing the old woman's screechy voice.

'Be about five minutes,' she screeched, as she waddled off in the direction of the kitchen.

Fifteen long minutes later, the old, toothless woman placed his so-called best English breakfast in London on his table along with a side order of toast.

Having eaten the breakfast and already regretting it, Allocco paid up and set out for Scotland Yard.

On the way, he stopped at a newspaper stand, where he purchased a Daily Mail. The front page was headlined:

Another 12 months of pay freeze misery for workers, while bosses enjoy a huge 53% salary increase.

That's capitalism for you, thought Allocco, as he tucked the paper under his arm and headed toward the nearest underground station.

Having eventually found the right platform and boarded the train, Allocco took a seat in the unusually quiet carriage. Apart from himself, the were only six other occupants. One was a young, pregnant girl, whom Allocco thought was probably not even old enough to have sex, let alone a baby.

At the opposite end of the carriage were three black, teenage boys and two very young white girls, one of whom was chewing on some pink bubble-gum fervently. She reminded Allocco of the cows his uncle back in Italy used to keep, chewing on the fresh meadow grass.

'What are you looking at, man?' One of the black youths shouted at Allocco, approaching him with his little gang trailing behind him.

Allocco ignored him.

'I said, what are you looking at, old man, do you want to do my bitch, you pervert?' The kid said, suddenly pulling out a hunting knife. 'Do you want some of this, perv?' said the kid, as he thrust the blade towards Allocco.

Allocco's quick reactions were more than a match for the young, black youth. Within seconds two the kid was face-down on the floor, with Allocco's left shin trapping his neck on the floor. Allocco, now holding the knife, pointed it toward the other youths. 'Do I need to use this?' he asked them, calmly. They all simultaneously shook their heads, taking a step backwards, before and retreating to the other end of the carriage.

CHAPTER 19

Scotland Yard, 10.45 hours.

Relieved that he had finally made it to the Yard after handing the young, black, knife-wielding thug over to the transport police, Antonio made his way to chief Baxter's office.

On entering, he was surprised to see a female sitting at Chief Baxter's desk.

'Ah, Chief Allocco, I presume? Hi, I'm Detective Sergeant Yvonne Slouch,' said the young female officer, as she stood and offered her outstretched hand, a slightly nervous smile upon her face.

Feeling a little confused as to why she was sitting at Chief Baxter's desk, Allocco shook the sergeant's hand. 'Where, might I ask, is Chief Baxter?'

'Unfortunately, there have been quite a few developments overnight, and the chief inspector is currently indisposed. I have been asked to take you up to the chief super intendant's office as soon as you arrive. Shall we?' She gestured toward the door.

They took the lift together, and made their way to the chief super's office in silence.

As they approached his office, they could hear a raised voice, 'How the hell did this happen? To Baxter of all people,' came the voice from within. Slightly embarrassed, Sergeant Slouch knocked on the chief super's door.

'Wait,' said a terse, angry voice from within.

Two long and embarrassing minutes or so later, Slouch and Allocco were finally given permission to enter.

'Ah, Detective Sergeant Slouch and Chief Inspector Allocco, our Italian colleague, from Turin. This is the police commissioner,' said the chief super, who was looking rather red faced and slightly pissed off at the commissioner sitting before him. He rose from his chair.

'Well, I'll be on my way, Chief. Please keep me updated on the situation. I want to hear about any developments from you first, not the Press Association,' He said sarcastically, as he exited the office.

The Chief super, still looking hot under the collar, invited Slouch and Allocco to sit down, before filling them in on the previous evening's events.

'As a result of Chief Baxter's disappearance, I now find myself without a senior investigating officer, or at least, not one with enough knowledge of our man Alex Langdon. So, I have sought permission from both our police commissioner, whom you have just met, and your equivalent in Turin, Chief Allocco. They have agreed to you staying on in London and heading up the investigation from here on in, or at least until we find Chief Baxter or catch this Alex fellow. Provided, that is, you agree to take the job. Chief Super Tingy said, almost pleadingly.

Allocco considered the proposition for a moment. Then scratched his head, before asking, 'Will I have complete autonomy? And who will be my assistant detective?' he asked.

'Detective Sergeant Slouch here will be your partner on this one. As Chief Baxter's partner, she is fully up to date with the case. Are you not, Sergeant?' Chief Super Tingy looked expectantly at the young detective sergeant.

'Yes, Sir, fully,' replied the sergeant, with a nod.

'Good. Well, I want a bi-hourly briefing on this case, even if it has to be over the phone. Starting at 13.00 hours,' said Tingy, waving them towards the office door in dismissal.

CHAPTER 20

15 Beverley Gardens

As Alex watched as things developed across the road at the safe house. He was still undecided as to what he should do with super cop Baxter. Should he could just kill him now and chuck him in the cellar with the now fairly smelly OAP's? Or, use him as a bargaining chip to get his hands-on Ben. He decided that the latter option was much more interesting. Plus, he could humiliate Baxter a little before killing him, which he would enjoy.

Alex left his post and went downstairs to the kitchen. He sat at the table and began to compile his shopping list, but was interrupted by the sound of the doorbell ringing out. Alex hesitated for a moment, hoping whoever it was would give up and go away. After two more rings of the doorbell, he realized that the kitchen lights were on, and that whoever was knocking could see the lights through the stained-glass panel of the door. Reluctantly, he decided he had to answer the door.

Standing there were two uniformed police officers, one of whom was carrying a clipboard. Both brandished their warrant cards.

'Hello, Sir, I'm Police Constable Finch, and this is my colleague, PCSO Church. We're sorry to disturb you, but, as you may or may not be aware, a serious incident took place at the house opposite,' he pointed to the safe house, 'sometime in the early hours of this morning. Did you hear or see anything out of the ordinary, Sir?'

'I am sorry, Officer, I was at a party last night, and, unfortunately, I had a few too many and crashed out at my friend's house. I only arrived back about an hour or so ago. So, I don't think I can help. Sorry.'

'No problem, Sir. Can I take your name for the record?'

'Yes, certainly, it's John-Michael Harris.'

Well, thank you for your time, Sir. Have a nice day,' Said the gullible teenaged cop, pretending to tip his hat, as the pair moved on to the house next door.

Poor kid, he thinks we are still in era of Dixon of Dock Green, thought Alex, tipping his imaginary hat to the officers' retreating backs.

Time to move on, Alex decided, as he watched the young cops walk up the next-door neighbour's path. He knew they wouldn't have any luck there either, as he'd seen the couple leave a few days ago in a car loaded to the brim and a ski box on the roof.

Alex stepped back inside the house and closed the door. Back in the kitchen, he attached the silencer to his 9mm, so it was ready to use should the cops come back.

Alex returned to the kitchen dining table and carried on writing out his shopping list that read:

500g PE

30 metres Det. Cord

2 electrical detonators

Second-hand laptop

2 PAYG wi-fi dongles

Pay-as-you-go mobile with sim.

16 steel right-angle brackets

Box of screws

Pack of plastic ties.

That should do for now,' he thought to himself, chomping on his last piece of toast.

CHAPTER 21

Ted's Office at Scotland Yard

Chef Allocco and Detective Sergeant Carole Speakman sat at their respective desks. Both were unsure about how to break the ice. The atmosphere could have been cut with a knife.

'Coffee?' suggested Allocco.

'That would be good, Sir, I'll go get us some,' Speakman replied, rising from her chair with a look of relief. 'No, please, allow me,' said Allocco, picking up his leather bag and producing his coffee machine, which he began setting up on the desk.

The young sergeant watched on in amusement at how seriously and passionately the Italian was making a simple cup of coffee. *Few, if any, of the men that have come and gone in my life have treated me with such passion, let alone a coffee machine,* she reflected sadly, as she watched Allocco level the top of the measuring spoon.

Coffee now in hand, Allocco and Sergeant Speakman discussed what they knew of the Langdon case so far.

'Tell me all that you know of our man Alex Langdon,' requested Allocco, leaning back in his chair and sipping with apparent pleasure on his freshly made coffee.

Carole thought for a moment. 'Well, he's an ex-Special Air Service Trooper, who's been highly trained in the art of counter terrorism.
His nickname in the SAS was Natural Born Killer, Apparently, he enjoyed killing people.
He fought in several wars, the first was the Falklands war of 1982, then later he was deployed behind enemy lines during the Iraqi invasion of Kuwait. It was there he earned the George Cross a gallantry medal, after he fought back a number of Iraqi troops whilst his team retreated. In addition, he also carried out several tours of Northern Ireland. During one such tour of the province, his unit was attacked with a proxy bomb, where he received minor injuries.

'Proxy bomb?' muttered the Italian chief, looking puzzled.

'A proxy bomb was a tactic used by the IRA. Usually they would take an innocent family hostage, then force one of them, usually the male, but on several occasions they used the females of the household, and would basically strap the individual into a vehicle laden with explosives, so they had no chance of escaping, and threaten to kill the rest of the family if the individual fail to do what they wanted,' Speakman explained.

'Langdon met our man Ben,' she pointed to a picture of Ben that lay on the desk between them, 'on the SAS training course. Apparently, the two of them worked very closely together as part of a four-man team. They became so close that they both left the forces in 1992 and immediately joined a private security firm, Valah International.

According to Ben, they were mainly deployed as CPO's for...'

Allocco held up his hand, cutting her with another look of confusion. 'CPO?' he said.

'CPO being a Close Protection Officer, or bodyguard to you and me,' the sergeant explained.

'Again, according to Ben, not long after the events of 9/11 they were recruited by joint UK/US Forces Military Command to carry out a highly sensitive seek and destroy mission in Afghanistan.

'The operation went bad, and three of the six-man team where killed. Alex was captured and held hostage for almost three years, before being rescued during a Royal Marine assault mission.

'Not happy about Ben and Stan Buxton, he was the other member of the team that got away, and who we later found dead on a remote farm in Essex. The thinking is that he was killed for breaking the so-called Code of Honour that says you should never leave a man behind,' Speakman paused, as Allocco nodded his understanding. 'So, it's likely that Langdon is seeking revenge. He's already killed Stan Buxton, Detective Annie Harris, and several other people who have gotten in his way, as you know.' Speakman took an appreciative sip of coffee before continuing.

'As of sometime in the early hours of this morning, he attacked the safe house where Ben was being held, killing two TSG officers and possibly abducting or killing Ben Hickson and Chief Super Baxter. We don't know, but both are missing. And, that's all I have right now.' Speakman took a deep breath, and another sip of her coffee.

Just then, the phone on Ted's desk rang. Allocco picked it up.

'Chief Allocco speaking.'

'Chief, it's Max Tingy. I need you and Sergeant Speakman in my office asap. T There's been a development.'

CHAPTER 22

16 Beverley Gardens

Alex lined up the front facing camera of the second-hand laptop. *Perfect* he thought to himself, admiring the image of Ted Baxter stark bollock-naked and tied to the chair, which he'd earlier bolted to the floor in the centre of the upstairs bedroom. The chair also had enough plastic explosive attached to its underside to blow up half of Golder's Green.

Once he was happy that the public would have a decent enough view, Alex hit the enter button, sending the live feed to View Tube.

After completing his security checks of the house and setting the front door booby trap, Alex exited the house via the back door, locking up behind himself. He then made his way to his new safe house, which was conveniently located just a few doors down the road. He had noticed during his observation of Ben's safe house that number 8 was occupied by a single female in her early thirties. Judging her dress code, she was a goth and, Alex suspected, probably into the dark side of life. Alex had assumed from her very infrequent and short trips out, that she either worked from home or was currently unemployed, meaning that there was a good chance that no one would miss her for a few days. He had also noticed that she hadn't had any visitors during the time that Alex had been monitoring her house, making it an ideal observation point from which to observe number 25.

Alex smiled, as he rang the doorbell of the goth's house. The chimes were one of those stupid musical ones that played a tune, this time, part of the theme tune to the Addams Family TV show.

There was no reply, so Alex rang the bell for a second time. A few seconds later, he heard the young woman's voice from within.

'Hold your bloody horses, I'm coming. Don't be so…'

The goth opened the door, when her face immediately met Alex's clenched fist, which knocked her clean out.

Well, that was easy, Thought Alex, as he dragged her inert body into the lounge and began to tie her up and gag her.

Alex looked down at the young goth. Ignoring the blood splattered nose, Alex noticed that she was actually quite good looking and seemed fairly fit.

Nice arse and pert little tits, he thought, bungling her into the under-stair cupboard.

CHAPTER 23

Scotland Yard

Back at Scotland yard, Chief Allocco, Chief Superintendent Tingy, Detective Sergeant Speakman, the Commissioner and Jake Cummings where all gathered around and staring at the chief super's computer screen.

The image showed Chief Inspector Baxter, naked and tied to a chair, which seemed to have some sort of a device attached to it, probably a bomb, they all thought.

'Once again, People, we seem to be in a bit of a pickle. This man Alex Langdon is pissing me right off, and I want the bastard caught or killed, I don't care which at this moment in time. But it needs sorting, and damned well quick. Preferably before we lose Chief Baxter. After all, I don't think I need to remind you all about what happened to Annie Harris.' said the irate commissioner.

'We now know that Chief Baxter is alive, at least for now. However, we don't know the whereabouts or the state of health of Ben Hickson. He's either dead and buried or also being held captive.'

Allocco put up his hand, as if asking for permission to speak.

'Yes, Chief Allocco.'

'There is a third possibility, also. He may well have escaped and is in hiding.'

'Or,' the commissioner added, 'as chief Allocco says, he could be in hiding.'

'Jake, get hold of that SISI guy, what's his name?' said Tingy.

'Danny, Danny Bradshaw,' replied Jake.

'Yes, that's him. Get hold of him and put him on the team. He's got plenty of experience of dealing with this sicko. He might have some ideas as to how to find where Chief Baxter is being held. Bob, you arrange for the BBC to put an urgent appeal out during the next news bulletin. And include a message to Ben Hickson appealing for him to get in touch.'

'Chief Allocco and Sergeant Speakman, I want you to go to the safe house and see if there any clues there, and get in touch with the usual border forces. I don't want this fucker slipping away again. Well, get on with it, People,' he said, dismissing the group, so that he was left alone with the commissioner.

'Now, listen up, Max, the Prime Minister is taking a special interest in this case. If we fuck it up someone, if not all of us, will be getting the chop. With two years to retirement I'll make damned sure the axe falls well and truly away from me. Do I make myself clear?' warned the Commissioner.

'Crystal,' replied Max, thinking, *'up yours, buddy.'* Silently, he watched the commissioner don his peaked cap and leave, then returned to the computer screen.

Having visited number 12 Beverley Gardens and gained no further intel, Chief Allocco realised that Alex must have had a local observation point, and so ordered further door- to-door enquiries before he and Sergeant Speakman made their way back to the office.

Once back at the Yard, Allocco and Sergeant Speakman were joined by Danny Bradshaw. They huddled around the computer screen to begin reviewing the View Tube footage of their captive colleague, Ted Baxter.

Allocco was his usual quiet, contemplative self. There was something about the room in the video that seemed familiar to him, but exactly what it was he couldn't quite put his finger on.

'Any clues as to where he could be being held?' Speakman asked Danny, as she crouched down to get a better view of the computer screen. Just then, the phone rang. Carole answered it before Danny could get to it.

'Detective Sergeant Speakman.'

'It's Jake. I just wanted to let you know, the uniform boys have completed the second door-to-door and haven't come up with anything new. Mind you, there were a couple of houses where there was no answer.'

Okay, Jake, thanks for letting us know. Can you get Uniform to send me a list of non-responders, please?' she asked, before ending the call.

The Detective Sergeant relayed the details of the conversation to the others.

'Coffee?' Speakman inquired, looking at Chief Allocco, who appeared to be deep in thought, with his eyes glued to the computer screen. He waved a negative.

'Right, I'll be back in a jiffy,' said Speakman, realising glumly that a special Allocco coffee was off the menu for the moment, so she made her way to the force's 'cafeteria' – actually the row of coffee and vending machines in the foyer.

When she returned to the office, she saw that the door-to-door reports had been placed upon her desk. Allocco was busy tapping away at his keyboard, and seemed in no mood to be disturbed. So, she decided to study the reports. Initially, nothing seemed to stand out. However, she did notice something.

'Sir.'

'Yes, Sergeant, what is it?' Allocco replied.

'I've just gone through the door-to-door reports, and I think I've found something that might be of interest.'

'And what might that be?'

'Well, one of the houses in Beverley Gardens is occupied by a man that gave his name as John-Michael Harris. Bit of a strange name don't you think?'

Allocco looked up at her. 'Does this man live at…he moved closer to his computer screen…, number 16 Beverley Gardens?' he asked.

'Yes, but how did you know that?' Speakman looked confused.

'Never mind that now.' Allocco said, rising from his seat and putting on his jacket. 'Get your coat and come with me.'

'Where are we going?' Speakman asked, following him out into the corridor. Allocco ignored her and carried on running towards the chief super's office.

Allocco didn't bother to knock, catching the super off guard. Tingy quickly placed his glass of Johnny Walker Red-Label into his desk drawer.

'Chief Allocco, to what do I owe this abrupt and un invited disturbance?'

'I think we may have found the location of Chief Inspector Baxter.'

Allocco explained that he thought that something was familiar about the room Ted was being held in, but that it wasn't until just a few moments ago that he remembered the net curtains in the windows of one of the houses opposite.

'I checked on Google Earth and found that number 16 Beverly Gardens has the very same nets.' Allocco said.

'Then why are you not out there, Chief Allocco?' shouted the chief super, as he picked up the phone.

Allocco reached over the table and grabbed the phone from him. 'Not so fast, chief super intendent, are you forgetting that Mr. Baxter is sitting on what we think might be a bomb?' For all we know our man Mr. Alex may well still be watching the house and could blow us all to hell! No, we need to think about our approach very carefully.' He said, carefully replacing the handset in its cradle.

'Good point, Chief Allocco,' replied a now sheepish looking Tingy. 'Sergeant Speakman, gather the team together, put Bomb Disposal on standby and have them meet me and Chief Allocco in the briefing room in fifteen minutes,' he ordered.

'Yes, Sir, on it now,' said Speakman, rapidly exiting the office.

'Now, Chief Allocco, let's get planning. We need a layout of the building,' said Tingy, picking up the phone again.

'I already have one,' Allocco told him, as he placed a floor plan of the identical house two doors down that he'd printed off the internet. 'All we have to do is to ensure that number 16 hasn't had an extension,' he said, smoothing out the plan.

CHAPTER 24

Serious Crime briefing room, 14.00 hours

The *chatter in the* briefing room fell silent, as Tingy and Chief Allocco entered.

'Welcome, People. As you are all aware, we have been working flat out to try and find both Chief Baxter and Ben Hickson. My guess is that they may well be in the same location. Chief Allocco will now brief you on his findings,' said Tingy.

Chief Allocco repeated what he had told the chief fifteen minutes earlier, then began to lay out his plan of action.

'There is a distinct possibility that our man Alex may well be still in the property, or possibly in another property nearby from where he is watching,' Explained Allocco.

'As the chief superintendent has just pointed out, looking back at this guy's previous modus-operandum, there is a likely hood that if, and I stress if, Chief Baxter is being held captive at number 15 Beverley Gardens, then Langdon is almost certainly has the house under surveillance. So, it is important that we tread very carefully, and that we approach the property from the rear.'

'What about creating a distraction, in the form of forensics going over the safe house again, and uniform doing another door to door while we slip in the back?' Speakman suggested.

Allocco paused for a moment, scratching his head. 'Yes, that might just work, thank you, Sergeant,' he said, then ordered Detective Jake Cummings to organise the uniform door-to door and the SOCO re-visit.

He also ordered Dan the SISI chap to do his 'signal blocking thing', then inspected the large map of London that was stuck to the briefing room wall.

'Sergeant Speakman, please arrange for the bomb squad to be on standby and to park up here,' he said, pointing to an industrial estate approximately half a mile from Beverley Gardens.

'I want everyone on the ground in one hour, and no marked cars anywhere near Beverley gardens,' Allocco ordered, before breaking up the meeting and heading back to his office for one of his special coffees. He also needed to make a call to his wife's nursing home, as he realized that he hadn't checked up on her in weeks, and the following day would be their wedding anniversary.

CHAPTER 25

Ben Hickson

Ben Hickson lowered the binoculars from his eyes and placed them on the passenger seat of his sister Megan's blue Ford Granada estate car, which he' borrowed from her. He was parked in a small road opposite the junction of Beverly Gardens. He yawned as he poured the last few dregs of coffee from his thermos. As he drank the cold concoction, he checked his watch, and sighed. It would be at least another hour before Megan would turn up with another flask and rations.

He had been there for the last fourteen hours, having learned via the car radio that Chief Baxter was now the one in one of Alex's special chairs.

Ben knew that Alex must still be somewhere in Beverley Gardens, because after Ben had done a runner from the safe house, he'd waited in the same street for a couple of hours for Alex to leave the cul-de-sac opposite. But he hadn't appeared. Therefore, Ben knew that both Alex and Ted Baxter were still somewhere in Beverley Gardens. It was just a matter of time before Alex would have to make a move. Hence, Ben's call to his sis, asking her to lend him her car. It was a bonus that she'd also brought enough snacks to sink a battleship. She'd also brought his special bag that he kept at her house, the one he'd used as a mercenary. It contained one of his old black boiler suits from his SAS days, a nine-inch, serrated Bowie knife, tag ties and, most importantly, his nine-millimetre Browning, plus ammunition.

Ben knew that if he was ever going to be able to live a normal life, one that didn't involve looking over his shoulder every two minutes, he would have to take Alex out himself!

Ben picked up the binoculars once more, and was about to put them to his eyes, when he saw a couple of marked police cars and a SOCO van turn in to Beverley Gardens. *Strange,* he thought, as he watched the uniformed officers disembark and begin to do yet another house-to-house survey.

Suspecting that it was out of the ordinary for the police to carry out three house to house enquiries in such a short space of time, Ben decided that it was time to investigate. He donned his USA black baseball cap, left the car, and walked down the alley behind the even numbered side of the cul-de-sac, taking a good look at the houses as he did so. As he passed the back of number 25 –the safe house as was – he could see two of the SOCO team chatting and having a cigarette. Again, Ben felt that that was strange. Why would they be there if they weren't looking for something? Then, he recalled how the SAS often used distraction techniques to get the enemy to look in the opposite direction. Maybe that's what the police were doing? Ben decided that if that was the case, whatever was going on was happening in the alley on the opposite side of the road. So, he made his way toward the top of the other alley, where he saw a group of people piling out of one of the houses, two of whom he recognised. 'So, that's where he's holding Baxter,' he thought. 'If Baxter is in there, then Alex must be close by, and will probably soon be making a run for it.' Ben murmured to himself, before turning tail and heading back to his car.

CHAPTER 26

The Rear of 15 Beverley Gardens.

All the operational team members were stationed in various cars around the scene, as Sergeant Speakman exited the garden of number 13, accompanied by an elderly couple. She gave the rest of the team the thumbs up, before handing over the aged couple to one of the plain clothed bobbies that had been drafted into the operation.

'Take Mr. and Mrs. err…' she said the uniform, hesitating, as she looked enquiringly at the old couple.

'Taylor,' said the old man timidly.

She nodded her thanks, then addressed the uniform. 'Take Mr. and Mrs. Taylor to Scotland Yard, and see that they are looked after. Anything they want, you get for them.' She then gave the old lady a reassuring hug. 'It'll be alright, I promise,' Speakman told her, as she helped her into the car.

While Speakman dealt with the old couple, the rest of the team piled in to number 13.

They gathered in the kitchen, where Danny was busy on his laptop, working on blocking the internet and mobile signals. Commander Godding and his team were drilling the walls adjoining number 15 and inserting snake cams. The bomb disposal guys were due any minute.

'That's it, all the adjoining walls have been drilled and there's no sign of Chief Baxter or any obvious booby traps,' said Commander Godding, as he joined the rest of the team.

'So, if he is in there, he must be in one of the two rooms on the opposite side of the house' said Jake.

'We can't drill into those without going in from the outside. And that will give the game away,' Commander Godding replied.

'I get that. But once we get the all clear from the bomb disposal guys on the adjoining rooms, why don't we break through one of them and then drill through to the other rooms?' Jake suggested.

A few minutes later, the bomb disposal guys made their entrance. John Godding recognised the young army c, as the one who had disarmed the bomb in the Ben Hickson case.

'Who's in charge?' asked the Army Captain.

'I think you'll find that it is you that is in charge for the moment, Captain,' said Allocco.

The Captain smiled. 'You're not from around here are you, Sir?' enquired the Captain of Allocco.

'No, I am Chief Inspector Allocco from Turin. I came over here to help and suddenly find myself in charge,' Allocco replied with a shrug

Allocco explained to the captain that his men were currently breaking through one of the party walls into the house next door, in order to be able to feed a snake cam through into the bedroom where they believed Chief Baxter was being held.

'Chief Baxter, that name sounds familiar,' said the young captain. 'Ah, I remember now – he was in charge of the King's Road job not so long ago. Well, I suppose we'd better get him out of there,' he added, as he was being dressed in his armed suit by his sergeant. Well,

Once the they had opened up a hole large enough for them all to climb through, one of the anti-terrorist team drilled a hole and threaded through a snake cam.

The laptop that Allocco and the Army Captain were staring at suddenly came to life.

'Bingo,' said the captain. 'He's in there, and he's sparko.'

Allocco looked at the captain in confusion. 'Sparko, as in out cold, unconscious,' explained the Captain. Allocco, smiled, thinking, then *why didn't you just say unconscious?*

'Now, let's see what little surprises our perp has left us,' the captain said, as he manipulated the camera's joypad and began scanning the room.

Allocco and his team were also staring at the laptop, not that any of them knew what they were looking for.

It was at least ten minutes before the Army Captain declared that there was just one bomb attached to the underside of the chair that Ted Baxter was strapped to.

'I suggest we all move back into the kitchen of the other house and work out a plan,' he suggested strutting off back through the hole in the wall into number 13.

'So, what do you think, Captain?' asked Commander Godding, as he poured hot water into a coffee mug.

'Well if you guys set about making a hole big enough for me to fit through with this lot on, 'he pointed to his armed suit, 'I'll get ready to go in.'

'Oh, and get the tech guys ready to block the internet connection,' he added.

'On it. Just give me the nod when you're ready,' said Danny Bradshaw.

'Then, I'll go in and unstrap Chief Baxter, send him through to you guys and then all of you must exit the rear of number 13 and a move a safe distance away. I'll the sort out the bomb,' the captain explained.

'What about evacuating the neighbours?' Jake asked.

'That would give our game up, and I have checked with the door-to-door guys and virtually every house in the street is currently unoccupied,' said DS Speakman.

'Sounds like a plan to me,' said Commander Godding, who then ordered a couple of his men to create the hole in the wall.

Ten minutes later, the army captain gave Danny the nod to block the internet access, then crawled through the tight hole and into the room. He took another look around before approaching the still unconscious Ted Baxter.

'Chief Baxter,' he uttered, as he shook Ted's shoulders. 'Chief Baxter?' He repeated the process until Ted Baxter finally regained consciousness.

'I believe we've met before, Chief Baxter. Don't worry, we'll get you out of here very soon.' He then explained to the groggy Ted what was about to happen. Finally, the captain removed Ted's gag, and gradually cut the ropes that bound him to the chair. He then helped the stumbling detective through the hole in the wall and delivered him safely to the waiting team. The captain waited for a few minutes to ensure that everyone was clear, before going back to work on the bomb.

CHAPTER 27

8 Beverley Gardens

Alex sat on the on the dressing table stool observing the coppers carrying out their door-to-door enquiries. 'I wonder why they're back so soon?' he thought, staring through the binoculars, watching mix of bobby's and PCSO weave up and down the house driveways with their clipboards in hand.

One of them was now knocking on the door of number 15. 'You won't get any reply there,' he thought, as he checked his watch. 'Poor super cop Ted Baxter only had another fifty-five minutes to live. That'll teach you not to fuck with the SAS,' he muttered to himself.

There was a knock at the front door. Then another, followed by the sound of something being posted through the letterbox.

Alex peeped through the net curtains just as the PCSO walked back up the drive and headed for the house next door.

Feeling hungry and knowing it was going to be a long day, Alex decided to see what the young, unemployed gòth had in her fridge.

Great, he thought, opening it to reveal all of his favourite breakfast ingredients.

'Grubby bitch!' he mumbled to himself, as he picked the dirty frying pan out of one of the cupboards. He went to the sink to wash it, but had to duck behind the kitchen cupboard rather rapidly, as a man wearing a baseball cap walked down the alley and passed the house. He waited a minute or so, before drawing the kitchen roller blind. 'Why hadn't I already done that?' he questioned himself. 'You're letting your guard down, Alex. Pull yourself together,' he admonished himself aloud, before starting to cook his breakfast.

As he sat down to eat, Alex recalled his latest disturbing nightmare…

He had woken up to find himself in the same dingy room he had left Ben Hickson to die in. Not only that, he was also strapped in the chair that he'd had built for Ben's execution and he was also stark bollock-naked.

He looked up to see a queue of people lined up in front of him. All of them had one thing in common with each other. He had killed them all. They were all staring at him with insane eyes. Each of them was clutching a weapon of some description. At the head was Stan Baxter. He was armed with electronic cattle driving prod. Behind him was Sebastian Poaplov, who was brandishing a broken beer bottle. Next was Annie

Harris. Her choice of weapon was a huge pair of shears, which she brandished in the open position. Her face wore a menacing smile, and seemed to be staring down at Alex's manhood. Annie was followed by the entire Maniceni family, all of whom were carrying scalpels. Behind them was John Michael and the French whore Rachel.

Super cop Ted Baxter was at the other end of the room. He had his index finger hovering over the switch of a loaded plug socket. Ben traced the electrical cord from the socket. It led to the chair in which he was sitting.

'Begin,' he heard Baxter say. His command prompted the queue of weapon-clad people to start to move toward Alex.

As Stan poked the cattle prod toward him, Alex woke up, shaking like a leaf in a swirling wind.

Tucking into his bacon and eggs, Alex concluded that recent events and his actions were now having a real detrimental effect on his mental wellbeing.

He would just have to put Ben's execution on the back burner for now. He needed to get away from it all and take a rest.

He opened up his laptop and typed 'flights to Brazil' into the address bar."

Following a quick search of the internet, he eventually found a flight that was leaving for Rio at 9pm that evening.

Great, he thought to himself. Only six hours to wait. He clicked on the book and pay button to confirm the flight.

As he did so, the whole house suddenly shook, and he heard the sound of the windows being blown in, followed micro-seconds later by the unmistakable reverberating *Boom!* of a bomb.

Holy shit! That's not supposed to go off for another hour! Hurriedly, he checked the time on his laptop. *The bastards must be over there!* Instinctively, he jumped up, grabbed his laptop and ran out of the back of the house and straight to his car.

CHAPTER 28

Outside of 15 Beverley Gardens

Jake took off his coat and wrapped it around the almost hypothermic Chief Inspector Baxter, before leading him out of number 13 and into the alley. He and Sergeant Machin helped Baxter climb into the back of one of the unmarked cars.

'Take chief Baxter to the royal Chelsea. And stay with him until you are relieved,' ordered the DS.

Ted, who was still very drowsy, was about to lay down on the back seat when he heard a huge bang, followed by the sound of debris smashing through the rear windshield of a car.

'Holy shit!' exclaimed one of the officers in the front of the car, as he slammed on the brakes and jumped out and ran to help the many injured officers. The whole of the alley was blanketed by a thick dust cloud. Most of the gathered officers were either stumbling around and incoherent, all were bloodied, some more so than others. Two of them were silent and lay unmoving on the ground. Shattered glass and brick rubble were strewn everywhere.

Outside the front of number 15 lay the contorted body of the bomb disposal captain. The force of the blast had thrown him through the front bedroom window. He was dead.

Jake ran to the first of the silent ones. It was young Danny Bradshaw. Jake felt for a pulse, but there was none. Jake made the sign of the cross upon his chest and moved on to the next victim. He knew its identity before he even turned the limp body over. It was Carol Speakman. She was also dead. Jake removed his jacket and covered his young colleague's body. Again, he signed the cross, just as Chief Allocco came up and patted him on the shoulder. 'I am so sorry for your loss,' said the Italian chief.

'A dreadful way to go. And so young too.' replied Jake, visibly upset.

Chief Allocco pointed to his bloodied ears and shook his head to indicate that he couldn't hear Jake's words – the explosion had left him temporarily deaf.

Minutes later, the alley of Beverly Gardens was swarming with marked police cars and ambulances. Jake led Chief Allocco to one of the numerous ambulances that were now on the scene, before informing a member of the fire brigade that there were two people still in the building at the time of the explosion.

'One of my men has found one of them,' said one fire fighter. 'He was thrown through hole at the front of the building. I'll send a team in to look for the other one,' He added.

Jake then instructed the police driver to get Ted Baxter to the hospital asap.

CHAPTER 29

Back at Ben's Car

Ben was about to open the door of his sister's car, when he heard the unmistakable sound of a bomb going off. He looked in the direction of the alley where he'd had seen the coppers gathered earlier, but all he could see was a huge cloud of dust. Poor bastards, he thought to himself as he sat in the driver's seat.

Ben didn't have long to wait before the black BMW slowly turned out of the alley that served the even-numbered houses of Beverley Gardens. He couldn't see who was driving, but he was ninety-nine percent sure it was Alex. After all, if a bomb had just gone off in their street most people would be running to help.

Ben started the car and began to follow the black BMW. The driver kept strictly to the speed limit as he meandered through the busy streets of London.

Eventually the BMW turned into a multi-story car park not far from Paddington railway station. Alex had an inkling that his man was probably going to get a train to Heathrow, and from there a plane to God knows where. He continued to watch as the BMW made its way up to the roof of the car park.

Ben exited his car and headed for the car park lift. The lift seemed to take forever to ascend from the ground floor to the third floor, where he entered it.

He pulled the peak of his baseball cap down over his face and bowed his head slightly, as the lift doors closed and began to rise up toward the car park roof. As the lift passed the fourth floor, Ben cocked his 9mm Browning and covered it with his jacket.

Alex, waiting for the lift two floors up, heard the very distinctive sound of a weapon being cocked. It was a sound he had heard many times before on the streets of Northern Ireland. The terrorists knew that the sound of a weapon being cocked in the dead of night could be heard a quarter of a mile away. They would often cock a weapon every now and then just to halt a patrol, which would often go to ground for ten or fifteen minutes on hearing such a sound.

Alex quickly ducked behind a nearby car just before the lift doors opened. He felt for his own pistol. Fuck, fuck, fuck! he thought, as he realized that he had left it behind on the dressing table in the bedroom of number 8 Beverley Gardens.

As the doors opened, Alex strained to identify the figure in the baseball cap emerging from the lift. Then it suddenly struck him. There was only one-man clever and brave enough to come after him alone. It was Ben Hickson.

Ben was surprised to see that Alex wasn't at the lift. Cautiously, he stepped out of the lift, and nervously began to search the roof for Alex.

Alex watched, as Ben's search brought him ever closer to the car that Alex was hiding behind. He waited for the right moment, then jumped Ben from behind. The pair fought frantically, each struggling to overcome the other. Both men fell to the floor behind a white transit van, grappling for an advantage. Then, a few seconds later, the crack of a gunshot echoed throughout the car park.

CHAPTER 30

Scotland Yard

Having been given the all clear from the hospital, Ted paused for a moment to look at the many bunches of flowers that members of the public had been laying at the steps of the entrance to Scotland Yard. He thought about Carole Speakman and how she had become the second partner that he had lost in just a few short months. 'I'll get the bastard for it,' he said out loud, before stepping into the building's packed foyer.

Amongst the throng of journalists was Chief Superintendent Max Tingy, who had just finished briefing the media.

'Ted, great to see you safe and well!' Tingy greeted him, rushing forward with his hand outstretched ready to shake Ted smiled back sarcastically, then reluctantly surrendered his hand.

'Are you sure you should be back to work so soon after your ordeal?' enquired Tingy.

'Someone has got to catch the evil bastard. So, if you don't mind, I'd like to get back to my team, Sir,' replied Ted, making his way to the lift.

Ted arrived at his office to find Chief Allocco packing away his beloved coffee machine. 'I will be out of your way soon, Chief Baxter.' Apologised the Italian, as he struggled to get his coffee machine back into his bag.

'No rush,' replied Ted, taking a seat behind what had first been Annie's then Carole's desk, and watching the funny little Italian pack his belongings.

A few minutes later there was a knock at the door.

'Enter,' both men shouted in chorus. The door opened and Bob Griffith's head appeared. 'I have something you need to see,' said Bob, entering and placing his open laptop on the desk. Ted leaned forward.

'How the hell has that come about, I wonder?' said Ted.

'My I?' enquired Chief Allocco.

Ted turned the laptop around so that the Italian could see.

'Is that who I think it is?' Allocco asked.

'It damned well sure is,' replied Ted, a smug grin on his face.

'Wait there's movement,' Said Bob. They all leaned closer to the laptop.

'Holy shit!' shouted Bob.

CHAPTER 31

474 Kings Road, Chelsea

Having shot Alex in the arm and rendered him
unconscious, Ben had bound and gagged Alex, before
loading his limp and very heavy body into the boot of
the Granada.

He drove to the rear entrance of 474 Kings Road.
Having seen the masses of crime scene tape strung over
both the front and rear doors, Ben knew that the
building would be empty. He stepped up to the rear
door and shoulder-butted it open, before stepping in
and checking that every room in the building was
indeed empty.

The last room he checked was the one that he
himself had been imprisoned in a few months ago. He
smiled as he saw that the room was still as it had been
the chair to which he had been strapped to was still
bolted to the floor, the mirror was still there and the
digital LED clock remained on the wall.

He then made his way back to the car and
dragged Alex's limp body through the house and up to
the first-floor former bedsit.

He then proceeded to strap Alex to the
homemade electric chair. The police had removed

the electrical generator and all the electrical leads, but that didn't bother Ben. He had other plans for his one-time friend.

Once he had secured Alex to the chair, Ben set about setting the scene. Using Alex's own laptop, he positioned the laptop before hitting the pause button.

He then slapped Alex repeatedly across the face until Alex was once again conscious.

'Hello, Alex, long time no see,' said Ben.

Alex adjusted his eyes to the bright light. 'Well done, Ben, you've finally managed to get the better of me. I would applaud you if I wasn't strapped to this. Then again if I wasn't, I'd probably kill you rather than clap.'

'That's precisely why you sat there. You were always a cold bloodied killer, but your recent activity, what you did to Stan and that poor police woman goes beyond reason.'

'Are yes Stan Buxton. Killing that useless piece of shit gave the almost the greatest satisfaction. He was an easy target; he never did have the right credentials to be an elite trooper. Not like you and me. We were a good team, I thought of you as my brother. I would have killed for you. That's why I was so disappointed with you when you left me to die at the hands of the Taliban.'

'I'm nothing like you Alex. Yes, when I was in the job, I followed orders and was responsible for many deaths. But on all of those occasions, it was either them or me.'

'Is it not the case here Ben? After all, if I were free one of us would die. Do you have the balls to see who that might be? Well, have you?'

'I feel sorry for you Alex. I know that you must also suffer from the horrific flashbacks and nightmares that I do. After all most of the trauma I have witnessed you have too. I bet you also wake up in middle of the night in a sweat soaked bed, quivering with fear after fighting of yet another ghost from our past?'

'I won't lie, I do sometimes. I often dream of being forced to put on a bright orange jumpsuit before being taken outside to and being forced to bow my head to make it easier for my executioner to chop off my head.

They used to tease me Ben. The Taliban would often make me dress up and have me bow my head. Making me believe that I was about to meet my maker. And the just kick me over and laugh in my face. Could you imagine what that feels like. Every time they did that, my hatred for you and Stan would grow stronger.

So yes, I have nightmares but I unlike a lot of our former brothers-in-arms, who use the PTSD label to justify their inadequacies I just get on with life'.

'Even if that means killing countless innocent people?'

'Oh yes.' Alex smiled.

'For a few years after that night in Afghanistan, I often thought about you Alex and wondered what had become of you. I even felt guilty for not coming back for you.'

'Why didn't you, my closest friend, come back for me Ben?'

'you know dammed well it would have been suicide to come back. The Taliban outnumbered Stan and I by at least fifteen-to-one.

'I would have come back for you, no matter what the odds were.'

'That's because people like you are born natural killers. I remember you telling once how you loved the taste of killing.

'People like me. Don't you mean people like us@ after all, we did most of our killing together.

'I'm not like you. I regret taking another man's life.'

'You relish in the fact that you hold someone's life in your murderous hands.' I remember I remember you telling me one night whilst out on a stakeout the you enjoyed the taste you got in your mouth when you killed. I also remember thinking to myself, that you are not the type of person I'd want as an enemy.'

'Was that just before I put one between the eyes of the dumb paddy in Newry?'

'Yes'

'I must say that was one of my best shots from one hundred metres,'

'Enough small talk. Said drawing his huge hunting knife from its sheath.

'You haven't got the ball's said Alex laughing.'

Ben rammed a gag into Alex's mouth.

'Oh yes, I have.'

CHAPTER 32

Ted Baxter's office

'Is this live?' asked Ted.

'sure, is' replied Bob with a beaming smile from ear to are.

A few seconds later Ben appears in shot brandishing his bowie knife.

'That's Ben Hickson' yells Bob.

'And I believe that that is the flat that Alex held Ben in. Replied Ted as he grabbed his coat.

'Want to come along for the ride Chief Allocco?' Asked Bob as he followed Ted out of the door.

All three men were now in Bobs car and on the way to the flat in Chelsea.

'What do you think we'll find when we get there. Do you think Ben is capable of killing a man in cold blood?' Asked Bob.

'I am sure he is, but hope to god that he hasn't. Not before I get the chance to have a minute or two with the murderous bastard.' Replied Ted.

'I would also like a word too.' Said the Italian with a wry smile upon his face.

Other books by P T Saunders

This Series

Left Behind I

The P T Saunders Story

Series

Cupboard Boy

Me and My Black Dog

Sleeping with PTSD

I Saw